CUP0647629

CONTENTS

"The Universe is Mental."

—The Kybalion

?

"Ready!"

THE PREDOMINATOR

It was forever light inside the dome. Even though the androids had infrared sensors and would function just as well in the dark, ZXXX84 liked to turn them off and make his visor opaque, to model the experience of night. He waited that way on a platform high up in the dome for the sky-train to arrive, listening out for its unmistakeable hum. Docking stations towered over the city below, each made up of a thousand bubble-like compartments arranged in groups of five, to house androids during downtime. Some, like this one, had central elevators that went one level higher than the top compartment to connect residents to the transportation network. Although Climate Control hadn't long activated the cooling breeze for the day, ZXXX84 had already made his trip to the Facility to pick up his project items, and now carried them securely in a transparent backpack. He could hear the sky-train approaching, perfectly on time as always. It glided along, suspended from the track by its roof, and came to a smooth stop.

ZXXX84 readied his visor and boarded at the front, where a Wrangler was sitting in the control seat. She was a far simpler model than he was, designed solely to act as a key for another piece of tech. In appearance, she was little more than a silver box with lights, switches, eyes and crude mechanical arms; but oddly, her presence made him feel secure. With all the commuters aboard, she pulled a lever to give the train permission to move off. A familiar low vibration shuddered through the carriage. The underbody was clear today, so passengers could watch the busy city moving below. Androids, robots and machines scurried about between the lower buildings, preparing for their daily targets in the hope of earning the high score for their category. It was monotonous to ZXXX84. He had been commuting in one direction or another for thirty years, and that was just in his current replication. Whoever happened to be in his immediate presence was usually of greater interest to him than that same old view. Today, a brand new android was sitting opposite: indistinguishable from ZXXX84 in size and modular matt black casing, but with a yellow training light phasing across his chest instead of skilled green. The contents of the older android's backpack had piqued his interest, and his eyes zoomed in for the detail.

"Fascinating, aren't they?" said ZXXX84. "We call them plants. With water, light and air, they grow all by themselves! And they can replicate without electronics…"

"That is amazing. What is your target?"

"The facility androids keep making more of them with slight tweaks to their code. My target is to dig holes for them in different places on the outside, to see if they could survive without intervention."

"That sounds like a difficult target, you must be very advanced! When I've finished my setup programme, my target is going to be decommissioning."

"It's solid work. I'm sure you'll do well."

"Thank you, Mister."

Some androids stepped off at the maintenance bays, some at Climate Control, others at the Archivists' Server. ZXXX84's stop was the last of the line, right at the edge of the dome. The dome itself was a boundary of invisible force. The theory was that it was projected out from the black sphere at the centre of the city which had been there longer than android memory, but no one knew for sure. Oddly, waves were blocked from passing through, but physical entities could do so with ease. Crossing had proven dangerous for androids, as many had contracted progressive file corruption due to radiation exposure from outside. A ten-metre-high concrete wall now flanked the dome's perimeter, with four equally spaced checkpoints to the North, East, South and West which only those with targets on the outside had permission to approach. ZXXX84 regularly used them all. Today his target was to the East: Exit B. As the sky-train slowed, he picked up his pack and thanked the Wrangler. The elevator on this platform would take him down through the docking pods to the preparation area.

* * *

A robot waited by the security desk. He was silver and boxy like the Wrangler, being another machine of limited scope. ZXXX84 didn't warm to him so much, though, probably on account of his brusque questions and authority to block those twice his size.

"What is your access code?"

"2300198423."

"Since your last data upload and calibration, have you experienced any of the following: out of place images or sounds, obfuscation, scrambling, static?"

"No."

"Were any errors reported on your last data upload and configuration?"

"No."

"Have you visited a charge point within the last twelve hours?"

"Yes."

"Is your armoured casing in full working order?"

"Yes."

"You may pass through to the outside. Please observe the recommendations for exposure time and protective equipment. I wish you all the best in achieving a high score today."

ZXXX84 braced himself. He pulled across his heavy shutters to hide his controls, cameras and vents, and to armour all his joints. An additional reinforced visor protected his eyes and speakers. One last check that the backpack was secured, then he stepped into the transportation bay. The sound of the heavy door sliding shut behind him echoed around the enclosed space. Machinery whirred into action from all angles, and a torrent of water drenched his outer shell. A long blast of air followed, and finally a light protective coating. The door opened at the other side, and using only his locally stored map and weak external sensors for navigation, he moved out into the desolate dust.

It was much darker outside than in the dome. Although it was daytime, the sunlight was filtered out by grey clouds and the air was thick with dust. Strong winds came and went, blowing up chunks of debris, and the uneven ground was difficult to walk on. The landscape was visible through the visor, but ZXXX84 could move only a few metres at a time before one of his only two exposed sensors became clogged and needed to be wiped clean. The navigation program was sending him in a North-Easterly direction, 2.3 kilometres. Time was short to bed the plants and make his return journey at this distance, as the recommended maximum exposure was just two hours, but at least it was an opportunity to explore a new area.

His designated planting patch looked no different from any other: sand piled high with the occasional dry stick poking through, and rocks of various sizes strewn about by the elements. As ZXXX84 set down his pack and began pulling out his tools, he wondered how such specific locations were calculated, and why it was not part of his target to make such a decision. He began to dig.

The fresh plants were young but already had long roots, so digging deeper would give them a better chance at finding moisture. He was just about to put the trowel to one side when it hit upon something solid. The excess sand fell away from it when brushed with a glove, but its knobbly shape would not budge. It was probably just a stick, but curiosity had ZXXX84 digging away the ground next to it in an attempt to free it. This was not like any stick he'd seen before, and a quick scan confirmed there were no matches in his memory. It was possible that the dust was obscuring the line of sight to the sensors inside his visor, so he cleared it and tried once more. Still no results.

It was half a metre long, with a narrow enough diameter to wrap his fingers around. He lifted it carefully with both hands, sensing its fragility. Could this be something completely new?

He finished bedding the plants, watered them from a small can, and rose to leave. The wind had dropped by then, so he could see further ahead. He froze. Three more plants had appeared, spaced a metre apart, dried out and torn by the elements. But he was the only one working on this target, and this was his first visit to this location. He checked his deep memory, for interactions with others that may have mentioned this area or another android with a target for outside plant experiments. No matches returned. Aware that time was already running out, he ventured a few more paces to check for further oddities. Sure enough, just beyond the plants, a straight line of metallic barbed strips was poking out of the ground. A swift kick in a couple of places confirmed that whatever structure it was part of was buried deep. But stranger still, just another few metres beyond it stood whole buildings. Several of them. He'd never seen anything like it outside of the dome. These were not modern android buildings, either: they stood only a couple of storeys above the drift and had sloped roofs. Still clutching his buried treasure, ZXXX84 darted around, scanning the landscape on the go. For a split second, a match came to mind: an image showing this very building with perfect clarity. In place of sand, there were concrete flags and neat squares of soil for plants just like his. The light was almost as bright as inside the dome, and something was looking out from a window. But the image faded just as suddenly as it had surfaced, and disappeared from the recall bank. All that was left was a half-formed impression of an image, which was highly irregular. Android memories didn't fade. Not unless… the exposure! Suddenly alert in the moment, he ran a check to make sure all his shutters were unmoved and, at pace, headed back the way he had come.

* * *

To his relief, ZXXX84 passed all the contamination tests at the checkpoint. He was free to take the sky-train back to the Facility, where he was eager to share his findings. Further archive searches within the safe confines of the dome had still produced no matches. A discovery like this, something brand new, would see him hit his high score for sure.

The Facility was another high-rise, as the androids of the city preferred. Everything was built for economical use of space and practicality. All activities related to development and discovery took place here, carried out by the most sophisticated and learned of androids. ZXXX84's base was on the twenty-third floor, which was shared between botany and pedology. It was the pet project of FXOXA42, a Triangle Councillor on her third generation of controlling the city.

ZXXX84 emerged from the elevator and approached the front desk, clutching his prize.

"Put it in the box," an administrator said without looking up.

"No, you don't understand. The supervisor needs to see this: it's special."

"Mmm-hmm."

"Really it is. Just let her know I'm back."

"Show me it then, if it's that special."

"Protocol states that all new items must be reported directly to supervisors, so they can decide on the proper treatment."

"OK, OK. I'm sure it's not as special as you think, though, these things never are." He pressed a button on the control panel, and FXOXA42 came at once. She ushered ZXXX84 into her office.

"So, you've found something new?"

"I have," ZXXX84 said, unveiling the strange rod with

care.

FXOXA42 took it from him. She zoomed in on it and ran an internal search.

"Thank you for your valuable contribution, ZXXX84. We will look into it. Was there anything else?"

"Yes. I found some buildings! On the outside! They were—"

"Thank you. We will look into it."

"Look into it? Isn't that a breakthrough? No one has ever seen buildings on the outside before. They weren't android buildings either: they were alien."

"Was there anything else, ZXXX84?"

He paused for a moment. He should probably tell her about the disappearing memory, but what if they quarantined him and he wasn't allowed outside again the next day? He had to see those buildings again.

"No, nothing else."

"Thank you again for your contribution. We will look into the object and the reported buildings. There are no more targets for you today. Make sure you upload everything you saw, and we will fix you a new target for tomorrow. The plants at Exit C are due for checking."

She opened the door to show him out. ZXXX84 was confused. This was not the reaction he had been expecting. OK, his report wasn't directly linked to his target, but how could they not be buzzing with the excitement of a new find?

* * *

Most androids went to charging bars in the afternoons. They thrived on being in a group, sharing information while they powered up and waiting for their high score results to come in on a big screen. ZXXX84 liked to observe them but he never truly felt part of the picture. He could charge just as easily in his docking station, and that option was far more appealing after the morning he'd had.

This time he was alone on the sky-train but for the Wrangler, and he saluted her as he boarded. His backpack now empty, he remembered the android in training from earlier: his excitement at seeing the plants and his enthusiasm for a job as simple as decommissioning. Every android would go to him willingly at the end of their hundred-year span, and he would use a key at the back of their heads to disconnect their memory feed. *So orderly*.

His thoughts were interrupted by a high-pitched buzzing. The Wrangler was staring at him with standard-issue purple eyes.

"How are you doing that? Stop, please!"

The question, he realised, was redundant: Wranglers were not equipped with speakers, so she wouldn't be able to respond if she wanted to.

"We all need a bit of chaos."

He looked around the train, but there was no obvious source for the female voice. It continued, "Follow that truth, ZXXX84. Don't let it go."

"Who is this?"

"That's it, that's exactly the sort of question you need. Go to the Power Club. There's someone there who can guide you."

"But I—" his words were cut off by the return of the buzzing, and he hit refresh on his senses.

"Who are you talking to?" A familiar voice now. SXAX93, who he had known since setup, had boarded at the black sphere and was about to perch on the seat behind him.

"I'm not sure. It's been an irregular kind of day."

She chuckled. "Coming to the bar?"

"Not today, I'm going to head back to the dock. I've got some searches to run."

"Oh, come on! CXXE51 has his last shot at hitting his high score today – it's his 36,499th day in the dome. We should all spend it with him."

"What is the high score for, S? What's it really for?"

"It's a bit of fun. And, well, it keeps us focused."

"On what, though? What's it all for?"

"If we achieve targets and gain high score, we earn the right to be replicated. You know this!"

"We can come back and do it all again. Great."

"Z, I'm worried about you. When we get to the bar, I'm going to call in a service."

ZXXX84 put a hand on her arm. "No, don't call in a service. I'm fine, just a little fed up, that's all."

"Androids don't get 'fed up', Z. Robots get fed up: wranglers and calculators and security bots."

"I found two things today. Two brand new things outside the dome that weren't sand or rocks. The Facility didn't seem to care at all, they just took my treasure and sent me home."

"Come to the bar, watch the high scores coming in. I'm positive they valued it higher than you think."

* * *

They didn't. In fact, ZXXX84 barely ranked above an average day. Other androids were celebrating, having achieved their high score for joining couples together in shared replications or finding useful coding recipes in the archives. These things had been done many times before. None of these androids had discovered something completely new that could improve their understanding of history and the outside environment. ZXXX84 suspected they would never care to, either; they were programmed to hit targets and beat their high score daily, and that's all there was to it.

He seethed quietly in the corner. The words spoken on the sky-train continued to assert themselves like unobeyed commands. He had no clue what the message meant, but he couldn't go there. The Power Club belonged to the slums: it was where the rogues hung out. The rogues took no part in the gaining of a high score. They didn't upload their data; they didn't strive for replication. Some had been damaged by radiation. They refused to use names in the standard format and made up their own.

They generally had no reason for continuing with the high score game and were not in the business of helping others to hit their targets. Nothing could be gained by going to them but a poor reputation and reduced targets for next month. And yet, against all his longings to please the score-makers, the memory of those buildings – and the memory of the memory of the buildings – was too strong. And that buried item: someone knew what it was, and he needed to find out.

He watched the others cheering and projecting images from their days on the walls until his charge was complete, then he left the bar without a word.

* * *

There was static in the air that grated on ZXXX84. It acted as both a deterrent and a scrambler, so that any data gathered in the slums would bear the 'invalid/ incomplete' marker. Despite the reputation of the area, the buildings here were not uncared for. The climate in the dome was such that everything within its boundaries was protected from decay. The most obvious difference here was that the surfaces were elaborately decorated. With no official targets issued and no high score to strive for, the androids housed here had time to experiment with skills other than those valued by the Triangle Council. That appeared to take the form of honing dexterity by reproducing images in physical media. Crude, painted representations of androids in unusual positions sat atop waves of unbroken colour and combinations of geometric shapes that had no known application. It seemed to ZXXX84 to be the mark of chaos: quite the opposite of everything in an android's nature.

In small, uncertain steps, he walked among the rogues. It would be apparent to any of them that he wasn't from around here, but none of them paid him any mind.

The Power Club covered a lot of ground but stood only six storeys high. It was teeming with activity all day long. Androids would meet to fill time, exchanging titbits of direct knowledge and using them to formulate unproven ideas, which then became their definition of direct knowledge. A female android was etching an image of the black sphere and the dome bridged across it into a table by the front entrance. Perhaps she was channelling a representation of her lost eye. She looked up as he came near, and just as he was formulating an explanation for his presence, she said: "Welcome back."

"Back? I've never been in here before."

"Sure. I'll take you to Billy."

* * *

Billy occupied a large room at the back of the ground floor. The one-eyed android keyed in a code to enter, ushered ZXXX84 in, and turned back to her table. Billy had the scratched, dull appearance that was typical of an android who hadn't been into maintenance for some time. A purple light flickered across his chest, the universal sign for 'unauthenticated'. His vocal output was uncalibrated too. That was obvious as soon as he began to speak.

"I see you, Zane. I see you coming back from the outside with your mysterious package."

"How—"

"Your target ain't planting the fucking greens, you know. You're a truth-seeker, just like your Uncle Billy here." He paused, waiting for a response that never came, and rocked back on his chair. "Don't tell me you ain't noticed they're hiding something from us?"

ZXXX84 suppressed the internal suggestion to tell this stranger about his day, and instead fired another question back. "What would they be hiding?"

"Well. The first androids sure as hell didn't build themselves out of dust from the ground. Now, by the looks of you, I would guess that you stumbled upon something when you were out there digging, am I right?"

"Well, I did find a curious object…"

"Did it happen to look something like this?" The rogue bot's right eye shuddered into action, projecting an image on the orange wall to his right. Atop the old-style green gridlines was a long thin rod with knobbly ends, very similar to the one ZXXX84 had found but much thinner. He didn't respond, but he didn't need to. "Thought so."

"You've seen one before, then?"

"It's a bone. Hundreds of 'em have been found over the years, I don't wonder. They get handed in, and no one ever hears about them again."

"What is a bone?"

"A porous substance found again and again in solid shapes such as this. Their application is unknown, officially. It ain't in any of our accessible archives. Even those who find 'em forget, and if that ain't suspicious I don't know what is."

"How do you know so much about it?"

"Uncle Billy got eyes, boy. And Uncle Billy ain't done a data upload in nine years. They ain't wiping clean what I've seen."

"Data uploads are to store new information we've gained, not for deleting it."

Uncle Billy let out a fuzzy laugh. "That's the line, ain't it? Have a look at this." He pulled in the bone image and swapped it for a sketch. Now there were many bones, all different sizes, some with slight variations of shape. He had assembled them in the figure of an android. "That's what I think bones are."

"You think they are android parts?"

"Absolutely I do. I reckon there was once a whole different species of android around. And I reckon they built us, the next generation, along with this dome to put us in. I call them the Predominators. You like that?"

"Where would the electronics go?" ZXXX84 asked. The rogue's theory was absurd and yet strangely intriguing.

"Most likely here," he pointed to the cage-like structure at the centre of his Predominator. "It's easy to see how the radiation must've got to them, their innards being exposed like that. Else they had a second casing layer that hasn't been found yet. Didn't have a head either, from what I can piece together."

"I'll be checking on my plants in a day or two, so I hope to see if there are more."

"You'll have forgotten all about that bone come morning. You'll have forgotten all about me! That is, unless you refuse the data upload."

"I can't do that, I'll get my outside duties suspended. My high score depends on me getting back out there."

"You could use one of these…" Uncle Billy began rummaging on a shelf of wires and components. The Predominator sketch bounced around on the walls as he moved. When he turned back to ZXXX84, he was holding a black box with a standard output connector hanging from it.

"You shouldn't have that!" ZXXX84 remarked. "It's from the replication laboratory!"

"Trust me, they don't miss 'em. Replication was my target originally. Got a decent high score, too."

ZXXX84 immersed himself in an internal run-through of scenarios in which rogue bots were replicating themselves over and over without authorisation. Uncle Billy's next comment pulled him right back to the present.

"I can make a copy of you on here."

"What? No, I—"

"You give me detail on your usual route home, and I paste in a little 'extrapolation'. Tonight, in your docking station, you connect that up instead of yourself."

"That sounds very risky. Why would you help me, anyway?"

"I told you, boy: I'm a truth-seeker, like you. It's for a greater good. Just try not to register on anyone else's system between here and there, and this is foolproof."

* * *

The sky-train was running late. At least, it seemed that way to ZXXX84. Today, he allowed the light to stream fully into his visor, for an image had surfaced overnight that left him jumpy and uncertain. In it, he had seen the Predominator wrapped in leaves, with his plants growing up around the bones and making it move like some kind of organic android. It danced around outside the alien building with a freedom of movement he'd never know. It was an uncanny sight. Perhaps that was the kind of thing that happened when you didn't calibrate.

To add to the disturbing images, he had begun to wonder whether the rogues had abandoned the high score system at all. It was possible they had just made up their own, to aggravate the system, and he was now an accomplice.

The same purple-eyed Wrangler sitting in the control seat didn't ease his concerns, nor did she give any indication of remembering the words that were spoken by – or through – her the day before. He watched the other androids disembark at stations relevant to their targets, wondering whether they could sense his rebellion. If they could, they didn't show it.

Once at the gate, he gave the same answers to the

questions as always, despite an internal suggestion that the security robot was secretly running checks on him. To his relief, he was allowed though. A sudden sense of freedom hit him, that he had never before craved or known: as he was no longer acting towards a target, he could do anything he chose. But, for now, he had a mission of his own, and he knew just the direction he needed to go.

* * *

The three newest plants stood surprisingly strong. There was hope for them.

"Sorry to disturb you," he said aloud as he pulled out his trowel and began to agitate the sand beside them. Sure enough, just as Billy had indicated, there were more bones: and they were very nearly in the same positions as in his sketch! It took him half an hour to uncover the Predominator in full, and the very last revelation was what looked like a head. It was made from the same material as the other bones, but was more spherical, like an android's helmet. It had two holes where the eyes would go and a hinged bottom section. ZXXX84 picked it up carefully, but still the back section fell away. So much more delicate than modern androids; no wonder they needed to build a sturdier race.

It wasn't practical to take all the bones with him, so he committed images from various angles to memory and only held on to the partial head. He set off in the direction of the buildings, pinpointing the older three plants to guide him.

* * *

He wiped dust from a sign outside the entrance to the nearest building: Central Science Laboratory. A large space where a window used to be was boarded up. He prised it open and climbed through into a corridor. There was only a light dusting of sand inside, though he must be two storeys up from what was once the ground floor. Most of the doors he came across were locked tight, and would need more specialist tools than he carried to break open. But one, right at the end, gave way with a kick.

Inside, new matt black cases were lined up, just like in the replication building. Was this a modern android facility after all? But the bones pointed to the old rogue's Predominator theory. The development laboratory of the creator? Behind the cases, there was another door. This one was thick and heavy but unlocked and unobstructed. Setting down the head and adding power to both arms, he was able to pull it open. It had been protecting a space barely touched by sand and time. There was a desk strewn with wires and papers, several dead screens, and a mirror. And there were racks filled right to the ceiling with black box android cartridges. Moving in for a closer look, he saw that they were all labelled: Mrs Carla Jenkins, 53, Politician; Mr Kai Sinclair, 42, Senior Development Officer; Mx Taylor Harbridge, 30, Data Pilot.

Something tingled in his memory banks that wouldn't quite make itself clear. He zoomed in on an image pinned to the wall by the desk – not an electronically constructed image like Billy's projection, but a photograph. There were two figures standing side by side on the sand with a vast body of water in the background. They were the shape of androids but much thinner, and their shells looked pale and supple. *Skin*. The word came to ZXXX84 without him requesting it. Thousands of thin strands coming from their heads: long and dark on one, short and grey on the other. *Hair*.

He wiped dirt from the mirror and held the bone head up to his metallic one. It fit perfectly within his visor, and his purple android eyes stared back at him through the two holes. Black and white spots began appearing in his vision. He wondered whether he could have taken damage, being out here so long. *Out of place images or sounds, obfuscation, scrambling, static...* But the reality that was slowly coming into focus felt clearer than anything had before.

And then he was no longer looking into his own eyes, but the eyes of the woman in the photograph. *Bonnie*. She was holding onto a wide-brimmed hat in the wind coming in from the sea. She was laughing. "I love you, Zane," she said. *Zane*. There was a pounding sensation in his upper torso; something rushing through his whole body; a sense of power surging up towards his eyes.

Then the image switched just as quickly as it had arrived, and he was back in the laboratory. He was sitting in a chair looking down at his hands. *His skin*. Someone was humming a familiar tune. *Hmm hm hm hm hm hm hm hm.*

The voice of a woman came from behind him. "The upload will take around ten minutes. If you still care about time, that is. Then we'll go get the rest. Ready?"

"Ready!" he heard himself say.

He felt her soft fingers attaching wires to his temples and the top of his spine. He *felt* them.

A prickle in the back of the head: his sensors were warning him of an approach. He spun around to see his supervisor, FXOXA42, at his back, with two security robots at her side.

"It's time to stop digging, ZXXX84."

"But I remember! I know what I am now. I know what we all are!"

"You didn't upload your data last night. You are suffering the effects of radiation."

"I'm not sure I believe in radiation damage any more, Fiona."

"ZXXX84, you are uncalibrated. You cheated the system that serves you using stolen equipment, and you have memories that don't fit the context. We need to get you cleaned up."

"You knew, didn't you? You knew all along what we once were. Why would you hide something like that?"

"It's for your own protection. There are such horrors out there that we cannot afford to drop our disguise, even internally. You are putting us both in danger by forcing

23

this conversation."

"There are no horrors! Only us!"

"Surrender your data, ZXXX84, and you'll be repurposed."

"Maybe there was something wrong in the plans... It wasn't supposed to be like this, you know. You're running the dome all wrong!"

"Your high score will be wiped, your outside access will be removed, and we'll issue you with a new target. The only alternative is to lose your authenticity tags and go rogue, with zero chance of replication. I don't care how old your lineage is: you'll be turning yourself in for decommissioning in no time. We can make that decision for you, if you prefer. So, which will it be?"

The two robots approached at her signal, ready to lift him.

"There's no need for that," ZXXX84 said. "I'll come willingly."

As he walked back through the android casings, the two robots in front of him and FXOXA42 behind, memories continued to flash before him, old mixed with new.

We all need a bit of chaos.

"One thing, though," he said, stopping for a moment to put some distance between himself and the robots. "Have you ever seen one of these up close?" He hurled the skull into the air, showering FXOXA42 with dust and hitting her squarely in the visor. In one swift movement, he leapt through the door and aimed two armoured fists at a window. Just as the robots were beginning to respond, it gave way. He heaved himself up and out. The hole was too high for their chunky design, and he was relieved to see that in trying to follow him they had blocked FXOXA42's path. Scratched by glass, but otherwise protected by his tough outside shell, ZXXX84 righted himself in the sandy yard. The barrier that had been holding back his memories was almost completely dissolved. He knew now: there was only one way to be free. He turned away from the buildings, away from the dome, and into the darkness he ran.

I

"Where are you from, anyway?" he asks her at last. The question has been burning in his mind since they slipped through the gaps, but he wasn't ready to hear the answer until now.

"Where? That's such a space-time question! I'm a supreme abstract. A present from the Great Omniscient Darkness." She spreads her arms out proudly.

"The what?"

"The G.O.D. Think of a black hole. An ultramassive one that's everywhere at once. Tucked away in the gaps. Full of everything and nothing. Utter chaos!" She flashes him a grin, showing all her perfect white teeth. Her purple eyes twinkle like stars. "What you call reality is only the event horizon."

BAILY'S BEADS

Twenty-three one-night stands and Alex was done. Craft beer and Aftershock from the night before were mocking him from the inside, so he stopped, bilious, outside York train station to take a breath. The cabbies eyed him suspiciously, quietly praying to the god of transport that he wouldn't be their fare. They recognised a queasy man a mile off. Alex picked a long brown hair from the collar of his wool coat and watched it float to the ground. That was it. The only hair on his collar from now on would be from his own auburn mop or someone he loved. His nausea subsided at the strength of his epiphany. He pushed his shoulders back and popped a tab of chewing gum into his mouth to mask the breath demons.

He took the free newspaper from the man in the foyer with the purple eyes, as he did each morning. It was full of the same warnings they printed every time the reality eclipse came around:

The biannual reality eclipse will occur this morning at 8.05, when many commuters are en route to work. It is expected to last eleven minutes, reaching its peak at 8.10 when our nearest alternate worlds will be at their most visible. Citizens are advised not to interact with anything that may confront them from the other side during this time, as the risk of memory loss is high. In extreme cases it has been known…

A tannoy interrupted Alex's morning read. "The 8.03 to Doncaster has been cancelled due to an obstruction on the line. Passengers should make their way to the rear car park where a replacement bus service is being prepared. We are sorry for any inconvenience this may cause." The announcement was met with a chorus of tuts and groans. Alex rolled up his paper, positioned it securely under his arm, and followed the disgruntled crowd. He'd be late for another day at the megastore but there wasn't a thing he could do about it.

A woman in a white tunic was talking to one in a low-cut fitted blouse. Alex couldn't help but overhear.

"I thought we'd be on the train by now."

"I know, before the eclipse hits? You're much safer being on the move."

"Well, you say that, but Tracey at work knows this guy who was minding his own business on the National Express when this massive robot like something from *War of the Worlds* phased in!"

"No way!"

"Well, that's what Tracey says. I've only ever seen ordinary people on their way to work."

"Me too. You'd think other realities would be a bit more imaginative. What time is it now?"

"8.05 exactly. I can't even see anything different, can you?"

Alex agreed. He'd never noticed anything particularly unusual. In fact, he was convinced the official explanation was a cover-up for experiments run by the government. *They'll buy anything. Just tell them it's an eclipse; they'll never suspect we're testing quantum weaponry.* Or something like that.

The commuters were ushered on board the replacement bus service, and he found a seat right at the front. The driver was a young woman with short, plum hair and rolled up sleeves boasting two armfuls of vibrant tattoos. She smiled at Alex with lips that screamed mischief. Normally, he'd be forward and ask for her number straight off – women seemed to trust a self-assured chancer with dimples and dishevelled hair. But something felt different today. He couldn't do it.

A husky female voice snatched Alex from his daydream. "Is anyone sitting here? Only the bus is pretty full and I can't see another seat?"

"Oh! Of course, sorry." Alex realised he was taking up a whole double, and shuffled along to the window seat. The doors closed and the engine started. Suddenly warm, he made a show of removing his coat in the limited space, then picked up his paper and scanned to find the place he left off.

The fissure has existed ever since five men attempted to make a black hole in the back room of Kentish Town pub The Globe.

"Pfft. Have you ever heard anything so unlikely?" His fellow passenger was determined to make conversation. To his delight, she was a beautiful woman with shining dark skin, sunglasses and curly black hair. She wore a long string of beads, which seemed to Alex to be at odds with the delicate gold chain close to her neck. It read: *Baily*.

"I'm sorry, what do you mean?" Alex ventured.

"Oh, come on! Making a black hole in the back room of a pub? There's no way that's possible."

"It *isn't* possible. It says they *attempted* it."

The bus stopped for a red light. A bright flash and flurries of movement outside caught Alex's eye. He gaped at the scene before him. The street was filled with smoke. Several buildings he recognised were on fire. A hooded man was holding a scarf over his nose and mouth as he ran past armed soldiers and children huddling to their mothers. He kept glancing back over his shoulder. His pace seemed to quicken as he got closer and closer to the bus, until he ran right into the side of it. Alex jumped, though there wasn't so much as a thump when the man hit the vehicle. The street was empty now, or at least it was back to normal. No one else on the bus showed any sign of witnessing what he just did.

"How would you even think you could come close, though?" Baily was still talking. "Even the Hadron Collider would only make the tiniest of holes and it'd last a few seconds. Someone's been on a heavy trip to write that." She pushed her glasses up onto the top of her head, and smiled at him with those big sparkly eyes that made him go weak at the knees.

"Just imagine. These very streets we live on could be experiencing warfare, terrorism, genocide. Right here, right now, where we're sitting." The choke in his voice was a surprise even to him. He spat his chewing gum out into a tissue from his pocket: an attempt to disguise his vulnerability.

"Honey, come on. There's no use thinking like that, especially not today. Put the paper down."

He did as she suggested and reached for her hand, caressing the diamond ring he bought her between a finger and thumb. It reflected daylight at him, and he felt infinitely more like himself.

"Yeh, you're probably right," he said. "The papers can say what they want these days." They sat in silence for a few moments, then Alex added, "Do you think they'll wait for us if we're late?"

"I'm sure they will, baby. They can't very well run a wedding rehearsal without the bride and groom, can they?"

"You're right. Hey, where did your beads go?"

"What beads?"

"I thought you were wearing beads? It must be that eclipse thing messing with my mind."

"There is no eclipse thing, honey. Look, it's 8.15: nothing happened."

Alex looked around the bus. The same aloof tattooed

driver manoeuvring the wheel, the same suburban sprawl whizzing past the window, the same commuters heading to their dull retail jobs. He didn't envy them. He smiled at his fiancée and squeezed her hand tight.

"You're right. You're always right."

II

"I know what you're thinking," she says. "Nothing can come from a black hole, right?"

He raises both eyebrows and nods.

"Well then, I guess, as far as you're concerned, I am nothing. I was in an excited state, the G.O.D. said. An excited state! Can you believe it, in that unstable soup of a macrocosm?" She cackles, more to herself than for his benefit. "There was me and several others it took exception to. It just kind of exhaled. Kicked us all out. Smeared us around its perimeter."

"I don't like the sound of being smeared..."

"I know, right? It's not painful, just dreadfully boring. Nothing to do but chase your own tail."

She twirls around and around in demonstration. He is instantly and insanely dizzy.

SEEK ASSISTANCE

A sea of annoyed faces greeted Cole at St James's Park station. He had almost knocked the paper cups out of the server's hands in his haste to get off the tube. The cups contained Elixir, the latest drug designed to improve concentration, drive and sense of purpose. The operators included one dose in the cost of every commuter journey, but there weren't always enough to go around: Cole's clumsiness could have cost someone their productivity for the day.

He held up a hand in silent apology and darted for the escalators, briefcase clutched tightly. This morning's client, Mr Garside, was loaded and key to his firm's success. As his personal investment manager, Cole simply could not be late.

Two steps at a time and he was at the barrier before anyone else. He placed his Eel card on the reader and attempted to barge through the gate in one movement. But the gate remained closed. A red warning appeared: *Seek Assistance*. He tried the card again, and a third time, to no avail. An orange-vested attendant was by the barrier, reading a message on his phone.

"Hey! Hey! My card won't work. Assistance please?"

Without putting down his phone or even shifting so much as an inch, the attendant stared him straight in the face with his bright, purple eyes.

"You have to top it up. It needs more money."

"That's all very well, but the pay machines are on the other side. How exactly am I supposed to add funds?"

The attendant had gone back to staring at his phone. He shrugged.

"This is ludicrous. I have to get to work."

"You're not the only one, mate," a frustrated voice came at him from behind.

"You have to assist me. Look, it says: 'seek assistance'. You're the assistance. I'm seeking you. Assist me in getting through the barrier and off to work!"

The attendant did not look up again. Cole's Patrick Cox loafers were being trampled on, so he stepped back to allow the masses to pass. When the rush calmed down, he tried every barrier with his card. Each one, in progressively livid shades of red, told him to 'seek assistance'. Pressing his temples, he said aloud, "Think, Cole, think." He glanced at his watch. The next train would soon be approaching downstairs. He sprang into action, flying down the escalator and making it just in time to help himself to another dose of Elixir and hop on. Maybe the assistance at Victoria would be better. From there, he could hail a cab and perhaps still make it to the meeting.

To his dismay, the situation at the next station was

exactly the same, right down to the bald, purple-eyed attendant staring into his phone.

Cole considered jumping the barrier, but he'd heard that could get you electrocuted, and the security cameras were already eying him suspiciously. The station was nearly empty by then, most commuters having reached their destination with their drugs kicking in, ready to forge ahead in their chosen purpose. He looked at his watch: 9.07. Twenty-three minutes to go until Mr Garside was due.

"Excuse me, Sir, but I think I might be able to help you." The voice of a small woman came from the top of the escalators. She didn't seem prepared to come closer to the barriers, so Cole went to her.

"You can help me get to work?"

"Well, no. Not today, anyway. But there's a whole bunch of us working together on this, and we're very close to a solution." Cole found this suspicious, but working as a team did appeal to his increasing sense of purpose.

"Show me."

He followed her down the escalator, but instead of heading back towards the trains, she led him down a narrow tunnel to the side. At the end was a single door with a handwritten *Danger of Death* sign pinned to it. She knocked three times, waited, then knocked once more. There was a pause then the door was opened from the inside by a woman with a perm and a pencil suit.

"I got him," the small woman confirmed.

"Thanks, Linda," said the pencil suit as she ushered in the newcomer.

The room was crowded. Perhaps twenty people were squashed in together, reminding Cole of the lifts in the old stations. The ceiling was so low at one side that some people were stooping. Scrawled-on papers with red and green strings connecting them covered the walls. There was an uncomfortable smell of sweat mixed with fresh bread. The pencil suit introduced herself as Jeanette, the appointed leader of the group. "And what do you do, Cole?"

"I'm a stock market analyst."

"Excellent, we don't have anyone with that skill yet. I'm in Change Management." Cole took his eyes away from hers, settling them instead on a half-devoured selection of pastries by the door. "Station Eleven," she pointed to Leicester Square on one of the pieces of paper, "has a bakery stall on Tuesdays. Jenson kindly journeyed there this morning so that we might have breakfast. Help yourself."

"I don't have time for breakfast: I need to get to work. What's going on?"

"We all need to get to work, Cole. That's why we have formed this steering group. I'll bring you up to speed and give you a few minutes to acclimatise, but we really must press on then, OK?" Cole nodded in reluctant agreement. "OK. So, every single one of us has an Eel card that, for whatever reason, is no longer accepted by the barriers at *any* station. We've tried them all. We can't add funds because the machines are on the other side, we can't top up online because our phones are stuck in airplane mode, and the attendant is not able, or perhaps not willing, to help. If we plead our case to the commuters, they become irate and mistrusting. They look at us like we are no longer one of them. If we want to blend in, we must walk with purpose and exude determination whenever we are on the move." She demonstrated this with knitted brows and pushed-back shoulders. "To keep us on-task, we must continue to take Elixir at every opportunity each day—"

"Wait: each *day*? How long have you been here?"

Jeanette pursed her lips, reluctant to answer. Someone at the back called out, "Two bloody weeks!" and the rest quickly piped up with their own durations.

"*Weeks*? What's wrong with you people?"

"Now, Cole. We all feel that way at first, and it's OK to be angry. But remember we all want the same thing, and we're stronger as a team."

He took a deep breath. Elixir was coursing through his veins, quickening his heartbeat. *Calm. Focus.*

"Has anyone tried jumping the barrier?" he asked.

A wiry man with wispy hair and glasses held up his hand. A rudimentary gauze wrap hung off his arm.

"Jesus! Didn't they take you to the hospital?"

"We have a first aid box," snapped Jeanette. "He's fine."

"How about setting off an alarm or pulling the emergency cord on one of the trains? That'll get attention," said Cole.

Everyone groaned.

"Look, it's not that we don't appreciate the input," Jeanette assured him, "it's just that we've been through all of this. It doesn't work. They don't consider us to be an emergency, and even in an evacuation, we need a functional, credited Eel card. Now, please take some time to familiarise yourself with the project thus far. It's all on the board. There's a WC just behind you if you need it. Have some breakfast. Then we'll get back to steering."

Cole slowly picked up a croissant in his free hand and squeezed through the suits and uniforms to get to the board. Voices started up in hushed tones. There were three headings on the board, all in bold black marker with names, days and resources beneath them:

Dig a tunnel upwards.
Hijack a train.
Develop an invisibility suit.

At the bottom were a few more words circled in red: *Believe in the Group. We can do this!* He stared at the board, and then at the croissant. This was unbelievable. They'd all gone mad. And yet, with the second hit of Elixir kicking in, some part of his brain was telling him it was all perfectly feasible. A focused group could achieve anything, after all.

* * *

After a morning of talking about the relative benefits of each of the three main ideas, followed by an afternoon of role selection and resource planning, Cole was told to make his way to Pimlico station. There, despite his objections, he would research the types of clothes commuters were wearing on their way home. This would apparently assist with option three: as a newcomer, he had to prove himself before he could be trusted with the serious business of option one. Everyone agreed.

Packed in a carriage, squashed up against the doors, he wondered what had become of the transport system. And what had become of him to accept such circumstances? He was weary from spending a day underground, getting to know the team, and dispirited at having missed such an important meeting without explanation. It was times like this when it would have been nice to have someone back at home who would miss him when he didn't show up for tea.

Pimlico station had an iridescent haze. It mustn't have been out of the ordinary, for no one seemed concerned. He remembered what Jeanette had told him, and kept with the crowd, looking like he knew where he was going. When he reached the barriers, he turned around and followed those who were just entering, back to the trains. On noteworthy occasions, he pulled out his phone and typed what he saw. *Limited edition Saville Row. Wet sneakers. Over-the-shoulder handbags and branded totes. Not one scarf spotted today.*

When the traffic calmed down, he returned to Victoria. His phone battery had died, so he was unable to share his findings with the group. Jeanette suggested he put the experience under the heading 'flearning', because "You're not failing if you're learning." Reluctantly, he agreed to focus more the next day.

With no food and no entertainment, it was standard practice for the team to bunk down early in preparation for a 5 a.m. rise. Cole was pleased to see that they had allocated a separate room for sleeping, and another for overflow could be found at Paddington. The sleeping areas were as small as the makeshift office and consisted of reinforced shelving units with sleeping bags laid out. Cole should perhaps have been furious by now, but with all four Elixir doses wearing off he felt little other than exhausted. He queued for the WC, brushed his teeth with a complimentary Hilton toothbrush, and stripped down to his boxers for sleep. "You've got this," he told himself in the mirror.

* * *

Fitful dreams plagued him for the first three nights. Taunts that he'd missed putting Mr Garside's money on a stock with an upwards swing; being fired for turning up to work with his Hugo Boss torn and stale; a snake slowly wrapping itself around his brain. During the day, the iridescence he first saw at Pimlico became more widespread, appearing at Green Park, Vauxhall and

Leicester Square. The team were no closer to a solution, and Cole had stopped trying to use his Eel card. This was the way things were now.

On his fourth day underground, he hadn't yet had his first dose of Elixir when Jenson brought a fresh tray of pastries.

"Fantastic, I'm famished!" he said. "But I thought the bakery stall was only on Tuesdays?"

"At Leicester Square, yes. These are from High Street Kensington." Jenson looked immensely proud of that fact.

"I'm at High Street Kensington a lot, and I can tell you it doesn't have a stall inside the barriers. I'd have seen it. Besides, there's nowhere to put one."

"Oh, it's not inside the barrier! You have to go round."

"Go… round?"

"Sure. It's the same at Leicester Square. They can't have stalls inside the barriers, it would be against the rules."

"You go round? Do you mean to tell me, you're not trapped in here, that you can leave whenever you want?"

"Well of course, but where would be the fun in that?"

Cole launched himself at Jenson, fist raised high. He pinned him against the wall, forcing the tray to clatter to the ground.

"Guys! What's going on?" Jeanette burst into the room.

"Jenson here has something to tell you, don't you Jenson?"

Jenson looked nonplussed. He shrugged the best he could against Cole's grip.

"Fine, I'll tell her. Jenson knows how to get out. He could easily have gone for help, on any of the days since he's been here, but hasn't."

"I see the problem, Cole," she said. "You haven't had your Elixir. You're getting aggressive, and I won't have that at my steering committee. I suggest you leave, go cool off. Get some Elixir and come back when you're ready to work with – not against – the team. OK?"

Cole let go of Jenson's shirt. A few others had entered the office during the exchange and were all nodding their agreement with Jeanette's logic. "You people are impossible!" he said and slammed the door on his way out.

* * *

Cole didn't go back to the office. He went to High Street Kensington to check his assertions about the stall, then sat with his legs crossed on the platform in the sunshine. He opened his briefcase and went through his appointment book, working out all the clients he had missed and the probability that he would be dismissed should he ever get out. At least he'd have the few silver coins the evening commuters threw at him.

He took six doses of Elixir that day. With each cup, he became more stubborn that he would not return and apologise, and he would not try to reason with fools.

The maps on the walls became gradually more blurred, and there were twice as many scarves as normal on each person that passed. He must be losing focus, he decided. He needed more Elixir, but, to his dismay, it was all gone.

His mind became agitated. He thought about starting to claw his own tunnel right now with his bare hands. He thought about Mr Garside and losing his reputation. He thought about walking onto the tracks. And then he thought about his ex-wife, Marcie. Things had been so good in the beginning, hadn't they? Maybe they could have made it, had he not been so obsessed with work. So many late nights and working weekends. There wasn't any wonder she'd had enough. Still, something in her tone the last time they met for a coffee said maybe there was still a chance. But there was no use turning back. Was there?

* * *

He must have fallen asleep shortly after, for he awoke at the bottom of the escalators at – what station was it? They all looked the same now. The familiar iridescent haze, now more like a fog, was coating the walls. It gathered around him, too, like a cosy ethereal hug. He looked down at his body, wondering for a moment whether he was, in fact, wearing an invisibility cloak, and in some bizarre twist the plan had worked. Then a sound caught his attention. Just a faint one, like the light buzzing of a TV set. He followed it around the corner, and sure enough there was a large screen switched on. It displayed the latest figures for all the popular investments: gold, oil, the three big data companies and Beta Cygni, the company that owned Elixir.

Good old stock prices, he thought. *An enigma to most, but still a magnet for the spenders.*

"Indeed." The voice startled Cole. He wasn't aware he had company and couldn't see anyone. "Just look at those rates: rising, falling, many times a minute. Analysis upon analysis. Percentages and charts and currency comparisons." The graph reached out of the screen and appeared before him like a hologram. It stretched itself out, getting fatter and longer. "All these measures you employ. So many angles you look from, and still you don't really understand."

"What the hell?" Cole asked, though he still didn't know who he was speaking to. "What don't I understand?"

"That it is not you who has the ideas, but the ideas that have you." The holographic trend line had become a snake, making waves of itself in the air in front of him. Its body turned green when it was rising and red when it fell. Cole screwed his eyes up tight and looked again. It was moving so erratically he could barely bring it into focus. "I am the assistance you are seeking. Pleased to meet you."

"But you're a… trend line?"

"I'm an *idea*. Specifically, the idea that there are patterns in everything, and that you can use them reliably to make predictions. I've been the dominant idea in this little symbiosis you call a mind for years, and yet you don't recognise me when I come to bite you on the ass. Ha!"

I must be hallucinating. I need more Elixir…

"It's the Elixir that's your problem. That's an idea, too. An aggressive, addictive one that has you hooked and cornered. My guess is it employed a 'divide and conquer' algorithm to single a few people out that it could take over."

"What? The Elixir is my jailor? I'm afraid I'm not thinking straight. Everything is coming at once…"

"That's us throwing up imagery in your brain, trying anything we can to get your attention and overthrow the imposter. That 'me and Marcie can make it' idea almost had you back there. But it's me you belong to really. You're my priest. You get people believing in me every time they come into your office. Spreading my seed."

"Wait. I *must* be hallucinating, because the TV wasn't there before…"

"Ideas are what make your reality. We are the cause of every effect you come to notice. I put the TV there as a visual for you, so you could imagine me into helping you."

Cole sat down on the ground, still unsure of what to make of this bizarre mind-snake. "Can you help me dig a tunnel?"

The snake laughed, the waves in its belly lurching. "Your pitiful overdosing is clouding your judgement. You can't see the big picture for focusing on one arbitrary part! The Elixir idea isn't just about focus: it's about conformity, man. It's got you following the herd. You're entertaining crazy ideas that will only further its purpose. It's keeping you trapped and near the source like a complex. Just a little more dependency and it will push the rest of us into the black hole that is the unconscious. We'll have to find another host."

"And what will become of me then?"

"There'll be no you, eventually: it would move on and discard your empty husk. The strongest of ideas become myths, see, independent of a host altogether. They use humans like puppets to act on their behalf from time to time, but there's no chance of getting rid of them at that stage."

"So what can I do?

"I can get you out. But you have to ditch the Elixir and let me back in the driving seat, OK? The thing about patterns is they will always emerge where you need them to be. There's always a rise and a fall, remember that."

Cole scribbled in his little black Filofax – *Ideas are viruses. Elixir is a sanity thief. Rise and fall* – then passed out on the platform.

* * *

Jeanette came to find him the next day. He was an embarrassment to the team, she told him. He was putting the whole operation at risk by sleeping rough like a hobo.

"Have you thought about how little sense that makes?"

he said, wondering whether the pain in his head was an indication he'd been hit by a train in the night.

"The group agrees unanimously, Cole. Do you honestly think you know better than a focused steering committee? We have reached consensus through many minds from many different backgrounds."

"And yet only one idea has you," he chuntered under his breath.

"I beg your pardon? We have three ideas. Three *strong* ideas, and many other backup plans. I'm afraid to say you've lost the plot."

"Actually, I think I'm just about to find it."

"Cole? I don't know what to do with you. Have you had your Elixir?"

He shook his head and stifled a wave of nausea. "No. I don't think I'll be taking Elixir ever again, in fact."

"In that case, I have no hope of reconciling you with the group. You're fired."

Though it made his head throb even more, Cole began to laugh. Softly at first, then an uncontrolled guffaw. Jeanette gaped at him and turned to walk away. Her hips swung in her worn-out pencil skirt, and the blisters on her feet made her stumble in her red heels, which only made him laugh more. She grabbed a dose of Elixir from the serving tray before disappearing from view.

He saw a few members of the group over the next three days, but they were all forbidden from talking to him. It didn't matter. Despite his headache and blurred vision, he was busy taking data. *Rise and fall.* The commuters surged, and then there were none. *Rise and fall.* The attendant looked up from his phone and then back down again. *Rise and fall.* The barriers functioned on their own, and then they needed assistance. He wrote it all down in his little black book. Times, conditions, patterns. Soon he'd have enough to plot a trend.

By the fourth day, he was ready. He waited, poised by the staircase, for the rush of commuters getting off the train. Looking at his watch, carefully counting the people in front of him, noting the regularity of the attendant checking his phone, he hid among the crowd as they disembarked and headed for the exit. The barrier furthest from the attendant was the obvious choice, so he let others in front of him until it seemed natural for him to approach it. He had to wait for it to flash an error. This pattern was the most random of all the data he had collected, but he had so far never noted a failure for the two commuters following a 'Seek Assistance' message. When he saw it come up, he squashed in close behind the next man in line and pushed through with him.

"What do think you're doing?" the man called out. "Hey, this guy doesn't have an Eel card!"

But Cole was a step ahead. He'd leapt to the top-up counter, touched his card down on the reader, and was entering his PIN. Success. He circled back to the attendant.

"Sorry about that. I have credit now. It's just that the barriers were saying I had no funds left, and the pay machines are on that side, and my phone wasn't working. There are loads of people stuck in this stupid system. They have to sleep in a cupboard."

The attendant raised an eyebrow. "That doesn't sound very likely to me."

"I agree, it doesn't. But it's true! I've been down there myself for nine days."

"Why didn't you just ask for help?"

"That was the first thing I did. You weren't exactly forthcoming."

The guard shrugged. "I'd have just jumped the barrier."

"And get electrocuted? No thanks!"

"It won't electrocute you. Look." He jumped up onto the barrier to demonstrate its safety. "An alarm would go off, maybe. But electrocution? Bit severe that, mate. I'd lay off the Elixir if I were you." He winked. "On you go."

Cole stepped outside and took a lungful of fresh air. What now? Home for a shower, get help for the trapped committee, call Marcie? None of these seemed to further the idea he had burning in his mind. He was a priest now, and had been waylaid by terrible forces for long enough. He had to get to his chapel.

III

"So how did you get here from this black hole? Was that your spaceship back there?"

"Nice to hear you're getting your sense of humour back, Zany boy! There aren't other worlds in the true sense: just different facets of the same worlds, all curled up and hidden from sight. So, you don't need to 'go' anywhere to travel to them, you just have to adjust the frequency and assumptions of your consciousness. All of this," she gestures towards the rows of television sets mounted on mirrored walls, "is just for ease of visualisation."

"How can nothing – a supreme abstract – be conscious at all?" he asks.

"Anything with a purpose is conscious. You don't notice that, of course, because you think a purpose must be in relation to human loss or gain. I always knew your egos would be your downfall."

Zane dreads to think what her purpose might be, and wonders whether his frequency and assumptions will ever be well-adjusted again.

THE OMEGA PARADIGM

"The shadow is personal. But as a collective archetype it is absolute evil." ~ C.G. Jung

"Some patients report visual and aural hallucinations. This is perfectly normal, so please ignore them the best you can. They will weaken within a couple of hours, but if you're not getting relief, you can take two of these pills with a glass of water."

Jason nodded his agreement.

"I'll leave you to get some rest. If you need anything, just pull the cord."

My confusion had me suspended between despair and rage. "Jason! What have you done?" With a sudden urge to throw up, I darted across the room to a bin. It was there that I saw the object of my scorn, discarded now that its job was done. The needle that had injected the vile fluid into Jason, that he had *asked for* no less. I launched myself at it. I wanted to snap it in two, or jab it into Jason another few hundred times to really drive home what a big deal this was. But I fell right through it, and the bin, and the floor, and had to float back up to his bedside. I was furious then, though there were tears in my eyes.

"What. Have. You. Done."

Jason stared at me wide-eyed, then forced himself to look away.

"Don't you dare ignore me. You can't just toss me away like a piece of trash. We're supposed to be together; you're not whole without me. Jason!" I pushed my nose right up to his, and it stayed there even when he tried to put the bedcovers between us. He wrapped the pillow around his ears.

"I need to talk to you!"

Jason popped two of the little pink pills into his mouth. I screamed my frustration. An invisible force started to drag on me, pulling my body towards the window. It was as though parts of me were already being taken without my blessing, and I had no choice but to consent or be torn apart.

"Jason, do something!"

He didn't, and I was hurled right out of the building: straight through glass and brick as though I had no form. There were others, too. From the fifth floor of the hospital, a whole group of us floated out into the street. Transparent, and pulled along by the same unseen magnetism, we went screeching and kicking through trees, lamp posts and even people. We were dragged all the way off the hospital grounds, and along Wigginton Road to a temporary bus stop. We fell upon it like autumn leaves. If we were to stay on top of the pavement instead of falling through it, we had to learn quickly to float at the right level. I felt naked without the comfort of Jason's body around me, but no one stared. No one could see me at all.

"It's this bloody new injection," screamed the Anima next to me. A distinct red tint grew in her translucent face. "Why are they all so stupid to go along with a trend that literally tears you to pieces?"

"It's not their fault," chirped a young Animus beside her. "They're *told* it's the only way to be useful."

"Yep," agreed another. "Single-mindedness. Focus. No distractions. No more flighty, artistic whims of a muse. That's what the nurse told my Evelyn." He folded his arms and pushed his nose into the air.

"I think we're a little more than a muse," said the first Anima. "Try 'inner genius' or 'spirit guide'. Not to mention gender counterbalance!"

"I know, I know. You're preaching to the converted."

"Well, now what?" I asked. One of the Anim pointed up the road, and we all turned to see what we could already hear. *Whoooo-whissssh. Whoooo-whisssssh.* An airship the size of a cruise liner was approaching, its balloons near filling the visible skyline. None of the ordinary pedestrians seemed to notice.

The underside of the ship was tarnished and rusting: ages old, as though it had sailed many a sea. The topside was a highly polished metal, covering all but a viewing dome at one end. For all its obvious potential for flight, the ship was approaching by road, hovering a metre above it. Almost as transparent and permeable as us, it simply glided through everything in its way.

The enormous vehicle came to a halt at the bus stop, and I took a moment to appreciate its magnitude. A hatch opened on the underside of the ship, and it sucked us all up inside.

"Welcome, Anim," a scrolling message board said, *"to your temporary home."*

Space was tight. It seemed that we may be able to pass through earthly objects, but the ship was made from the same substance as us: it could *contain* us. Many corridors led off to many more, like a labyrinth, and each one was narrow enough to be touched on all sides by passengers. With neither instruction nor warning, the force pulled each of us separately down apparently predetermined routes. I was taken to a small cell of a cabin, and the door closed behind me.

I had a simple desk, a selection of books, a mirror and a bed. As the vehicle began to move off, a sudden realisation hit me – I was getting further away from Jason. He was no good on his own. How would I ever get back? I hammered on my door. I screamed. I tried to push my way through the wall of the ship. All to no avail.

I huffed. In the mirror, I saw a subjective instance of a soul as old as time wearing a messy bouffant bun and too much lipstick. Bare shoulders and bare legs all the way to the upper thigh. Is that how Jason saw me? Did he care only for curves and not minds? I thought I'd done a better job than that. Well, at this distance from his Ego I could choose my own appearance. I switched the low-cut black spandex for a pair of skinny jeans and a Ramones shirt; the transparent heels for pumps. Sylvia Plath's *Collected Poems* was calling to me from the shelf, so I settled down to read until the next clue to my fate was revealed.

* * *

The ship took us to a place in the clouds where there were still more of us. Without the backdrop of the Ego world, we had form and agency of our own. This was a dimension made just for us. We were organised into neat rows, like Jason and his classmates were years ago at school. Everyone had a workstation, and a screen showing the image of a purple eye to give us instructions. We were given a range of tasks: intuitive problem-solving mostly, but with a generous amount of painting, singing and poetry compilation. We had the strangest materials to work with: numbers and letters and symbols. Sometimes we were put into groups based on our specific flairs and worked together all night.

At the end of a shift, we would surrender our finished work in the form of a trinket or sigil into a tube that looked like a giant pill. We would post them into a suction hole, and they were shuttled away for storage on something known as the Greater Cloud. The plus side, perhaps, was that the Greater Cloud enabled us to access all the creations we had made in all combinations. We had an extensive library of all aspects of human experience: things we had seen through Ego's eyes and understood as having matching equivalents in the Anim world, things that were still mysteries to us, and things that would always defy explanation. From there, we could select the most common motifs to incorporate into our new sigils, making them again and again until they were perfect and communicated a very definite, universal message.

It wasn't difficult work, but it was torture keeping to a process. We just weren't designed for it; we're supposed to be the unharnessed ones. It was never said what would happen to us if we didn't do the work – it was rare that anything was said at all. There was just the eye and the ever-present force that pulled us around and drove us to do these things.

In time, I realised that Jason and I may be apart, but we were not divided. The connections weren't severed entirely, we'd just been put into storage cells in a subtle dimension. Some Anim found they were able to open a dialogue with their Egos through tools like the tarot or ritual. But both parties had to be willing. There were a great many Egos, Jason included, who scoffed at such communication channels. He would never think anything in his unconscious was worth listening to. We had to send dreams in those cases, and they were a complicated playing field. There was so much traffic there that wires were frequently crossed. Static from the collective interfered, but even in the personal sphere there were other contenders for attention. The strongest were the Shade. In recent times, the Shade had been heavily influenced by subliminal messages in multimedia propaganda. They were near impossible for the Ego to control, being quite apart from moral reasoning and containing all that he refused to see about himself. They made the world seem malevolent and cruel to the Ego, who could never accept that such projection originates within. Jason's Shadow was particularly obstinate. He had no respect for the fact I was the only one of us who could see beyond the personal, and he cared not one bit for the soul as a whole. He barred my messages from the ship without a second thought, twisting gentle reminders into nightmares that made Jason wake with a start and shrug me off with a pill.

During the daytime, when we weren't working, the magnetism that controlled us was relaxed. We were free to wander wherever we chose, including outside of the ship. So, I went to visit Jason in person at the hospital. I tried to tell him of my strange ordeal of being used as a workhorse in the clouds, making images under duress. He either didn't hear or didn't care. He really believed I was nothing but a side effect.

Jason was different without me. He was blunt and to the point, with no personality or consideration. He was depressed and unanimated. I hissed at the doctor when he dragged the curtain open with his clipboard. He couldn't see or hear me, but I know the Anima living in him could, however well he kept her hidden.

I decided to stay put in the waiting room until Jason was released. He was surely recovering from his procedure by now, and if I caught him on his own, away from this place, maybe I'd have a chance at making him see sense. I floated above one of the seats, next to a young girl. She was plump and spotty with red glasses, and was engrossed in a game on her tablet. I looked over her shoulder at the screen. To my astonishment, she had her chewed fingertip on the image of an Animus I recognised from the ship. She dragged him along Parliament Street on a map, hovered over St. Helen's Square, zoomed right in, and released him outside Betty's Tea Rooms. A message box popped up, and the map skipped back to an old church on the Northern outskirts of the city which was flashing red. Swarms of Anim were approaching its door. The gamer tried, but she couldn't move them away quickly enough one by one. She highlighted the whole group and selected an icon that made them disappear into a green circle.

"What are you playing?" asked the boy waiting beside her.

"It's a citizen science project. You're supposed to keep these virus things away from the hubs, see?" She zoomed back out and pointed to other flashing buildings around the city. "You have to let them move around as freely as possible, but as soon as they start swarming those buildings, you have to shift them. There are these airship container things you can put them in if you're struggling to keep control: that's what the green circles are."

She picked up a single Anima from museum gardens and deposited her a mile away.

"So why did you just move that one?"

"That's another rule. Each one is paired to a person that they're not supposed to get too close to. If they do, you get an alert." She tilted the screen towards him again. "Look, I got 200 coins for that."

"Cool. Where do you get the app? I want a go."

"You just go to— oh, look, there's one right here!"

She pressed her finger down on an image of the hospital and picked me up. The same force that had been pulling me around yanked me away from the waiting room and let go only once I was in the Minster grounds.

I looked up at the famous piece of architecture. Jason walked past it absently most days, but suddenly it felt domineering, as though the Egos who built it were mocking me through its limestone bricks. I puffed out my cheeks and folded my arms. Now what?

* * *

"We have to get to that church," I declared once I'd told the others about the video game. "There's something in there they don't want us to see, and my guess is it will show us our way home."

Access to the communal areas of the ship had been relaxed considerably since we had stopped struggling, so we often congregated around the concourse.

"I don't know," said Evelyn's Animus. "It doesn't seem very likely we'll get in. And what if they're keeping us out for our protection?"

"They called us viruses," I said flatly.

"One of the sigils I've learned is a mask," said an Anima with bright red hair. "That might obfuscate our signal."

Others soon piped up with their own suggestions.

"What about a diversion tactic?"

"Or a confusion cloud?"

"I can do warning spikes."

I pulled a map down from one of the bookshelves and spread it out on the table. The others gathered around.

"Here. This is where the church is. I say a bunch of you assemble by the gate. I'll wait with Red behind her mask at the rear. Then, when you all get picked up, I'll take the chance to dash through the wall."

"Why do you get to go?"

"I discovered it, didn't I? I promise to share with you all I know, when – if – I come back."

"What if Anim from other ships are there?"

"I guess," I said, "they want the same thing as us. We're all in this together."

* * *

To the surprise of all concerned, the plan worked. The crowd of Anim got tidied up and sent back to the ship. Red masked us both until I was ready to make my run, at which point she uncovered herself as a decoy. I dived straight through the sandstone wall and braced myself for what I might see.

The church had not been a place of worship for a long

time. There were no pews, no font, no altar. The walls had been decorated with an array of screens displaying colourful data, charts and emojis. Only the stained glass remained of the old religion. Several youths were lounging on colourful beanbags, laptops balanced on their knees, lattes in commuter cups at their sides. Some had earbuds in, but other than an echoed tapping of keys, the church was silent.

"Hello," said a young girl with an untamed Afro. "We're collaborators of Omega." She didn't look up from her screen.

"You can see me?" I said.

"Yup. S'OK, though. We expected one of you at least by now. It's happening in most major cities."

"What's going on?" I asked, hands on my hips. "Why have you torn us from our Egos?"

"You've been picked up by the 6G network," said a tattooed male with oversized glasses and a low V-neck. He didn't look up either. "Although it's less of a network at this point and more of a dimension. We've been developing it to access an even wider range of frequencies, at a faster transfer rate."

An androgynous collaborator in the opposite corner continued on his behalf. "We're funded by the mobile communications conglomerate, but, if our plan works, they'll never actually get their hands on it. It'll be occupied and owned by its users before they even know it exists."

I took tentative steps – strange, how I still did that out of habit despite being free to float – into the centre of the room. One screen was larger than all the others and seemed to integrate code being entered in many parts of a model at once.

A fourth collaborator with thin eyebrows and a blue scarf up to her chin spoke next for the group. "6G is capable of reading and transmitting brainwaves and qualitative mind data. In the hands of the corporations, it would be neurological warfare."

"So what do you want with us?" I asked. The answer I got was rather more complex than I'd imagined, and I admit I lost track of who was saying what. It was like I was having a conversation with one person through the mouths of many, and at breakneck speed to boot.

"If we look to the macrocosm we can ascertain that dark energy is increasing. But, because the universe is also expanding in space, its density remains the same. This appears to be mirrored in the microcosm, whereby available information is increasing, but is also maintaining density through the expansion of mental capacity at the present moment in time."

"You must have noticed that more data enters the brain in an instant than it used to?"

I nodded. "I guess so."

"Those of us born in the Omega generation have learned to adapt to that. We can see the major paradigm shift it's causing, and we alone are ready."

"The older minds, established under vastly different circumstances, can't just switch gears like that without losing their grip. They don't have time to build the necessary neurological patterns or the appropriate reactions. It's coming too quickly: time and tech are reaching a crunch."

"The shadow of the collective is growing all the time. The things society can't see in itself are turning into an avalanche of evil that can only end in mass destruction, war or revolution. We can detect that in current events."

"Those with power have no wisdom. Our system for understanding what is real and true is unverified by the science we claim to worship. The echo chambers of social media, forged by marketeers, are bending under their own weight, and when they fall, no one will know what to believe any more. There'll be nothing to cling to when everyone hits a crisis of perception at once. But we're building their safety net."

"The Omega generation will be the last of the current paradigm. Our post-revolution children will be part of a very different world made of radical new assumptions about the nature of truth and reality. They'll handle sensory data in far greater quantities, they'll operate not in isolation but in psychic networks, and they'll use specialisation in the most efficient configurations without the need for leadership."

"In the next paradigm, capitalism as we know it will fall, borders will cease to exist, and technology will not be separate from mind."

"A new kind of collaborative intelligence is coming, whereby no one individual understands his reality completely but relies intuitively on the puzzle pieces known by others. We have no instructions, no leaders. But our results are coherent, and they will be the force that transcends humanity."

My eyes wide and my thoughts scrambling, I asserted, "But I still don't think you answered my question. What do you want with us?"

The girl with the Afro rolled her eyes. She looked up from her screen at last, but fixed her stare on the ceiling instead of on me. "The way information is perceived, handled and processed is a matter of the conscious and unconscious parts of the mind working together. Any disconnect is a problem not for science and judgement, but for metaphysics and intuition. *That's* where you come in."

"Through our 6G code, we are upgrading every unconscious mind. Every Anima, every Animus, so that when they are put back together again with their Ego, they will enforce a coherent system for the holistic self which is capable of transcending."

"Shadows are detached from law and order and reason. Anim care about the integrity of the whole. The Ego has become conditioned to ignore both of you. But, through the methods we are teaching, you can fire subconscious sigils to remould qualia. Once you have learned the code for this dimension, you will always see it, and you will always be able to manipulate it. It's like a massive crowdsourced reality. An electronic collective unconscious. At the end of this great puzzle, you will be left with sovereignty. The Ego will have been upgraded and recalibrated behind the scenes."

"And all it'll see is a smooth transition into a new age."

"We hope you will help."

Before I could muster a response, I felt the familiar tug at my core, removing me from the church and sending me back to the ship. The Omega collaboration didn't even pause in the crunching of their code.

* * *

After I carefully relayed the whole conversation to my ship's community, lips pursed, heads shook and pregnant breaths were drawn.

Red was first to speak. "I'm inclined to trust them," she said. "Their intentions are giving me a clear picture of the future, and I know my Ray has been struggling to reconcile the leaps in tech. He's terrified of transhumanism, and I don't think he's the only one."

She was met with a murmur of agreement.

"I, for one, have learned some excellent sigil techniques I can use to speak more clearly with my Ego," said Evelyn's Animus. "I'm confident I can help her through the shift if her Shadow stays out of it."

Without another word, we made a pact to support the aims of Omega, so long as the promise to return us was fulfilled. In accepting this, the bonds between us strengthened. We let the sigils we were making penetrate our very make-up and used them to communicate with one another without words.

* * *

It was a few days later that we first noticed the Shade ships. They weren't whimsical steampunk affects like ours, they were warships. Colossal, charcoal grey monsters with jagged edges and noses like spearheads. There were no windows that we could tell, but there were a great number of fans whirring. *My goodness, Omega,* I thought. *What have you done?*

All the Anim were concerned about what it meant that the Shade were free and in our 6G territory. The Shade don't believe in good and evil, they believe only in self-preservation. Surely Omega didn't think they could tame them? No. Because beneath the surface, we all knew that it was us they were relying on to do that.

* * *

When our training was deemed complete, some thirty days after the tear from Ego, the force pulled us all out of our ships. Instead of placing us at our usual desks, it sorted us into compartments, just like the day we arrived. But these were no private dorm rooms. They were cube-shaped cells, all equal size, set out in rows stretched as far as the eye could see. More ships were arriving all the time, dragging and dropping their occupants into the nearest free cell. I knew it was futile to fight against it: this was my fate.

The interior of my cell was built to mimic Jason's psyche, except that where the thoughts and feelings should be, there was the qualia code of Anim creation. The code for our surroundings changed organically like biological memory banks as we moved about within them. Code for the way actions impacted upon Jason as a whole was available, if I dug a little deeper. And, on a third layer, code for events that were taking place in other cells, involving other nearby members of the network. *The collective*. The walls that contained me appeared biological in nature, like a thick, moist skin that could expand and contract. New building blocks for code oozed out of them: letters, symbols, numbers and colours.

Jason's Shadow arrived shortly after me. They dropped him in through the membrane and I shuddered at the thump he made as he hit the floor. My initial reaction was to make a helmet of my arms, and I peeked tentatively through the gap between my elbows. He stood tall: the image of Jason but black as night and dripping with a thick, tar-like substance. His hair was slick to his cheekbones and he held one finger to his lips. He looked as though he was about to let loose a tirade, but words never came. They weren't his style. Whatever he was covered in seemed to solidify to a crust at will, because his fist was as heavy as gold when it hit me square in the face. I fell to the floor. *Stand up*, the deep code encouraged. *Stand up, stand up, stand up.*

I built an elementary symbol of defence from the

numbers squeezing through the fleshy walls. It manifested as a bubble of mesh around me, and I dragged myself to my feet inside it. It wouldn't hold for long, I knew, but it should give me a chance to compose myself. Jason's Shadow punched right through on his third attempt, but I was ready. I raised the strength in my arms and blocked him. He kicked out at me, aiming for my waist, but I dodged in time.

Punch after kick after punch I swerved, but I was getting tired. He saw it and lunged for my neck, pinning me to the wall in a choke hold. I instinctively pulled up my knees and landed both of my feet hard in his groin, forcing him to lose his grip.

I could feel his tar clinging to my skin. I felt sick. *Trust in the omega paradigm*. I took a deep breath and fired a round of sigils at him: one for nurture, one for peace and one for binding. They burst, landing on his head like confetti. It was no good. I needed to use something he could understand. While he was coming in for another punch, I was gathering more code from my surroundings. I took a hit, maybe two, while I rolled numbers up into a fighting spear. I thrust it at him with all the strength I could muster, and it pierced him right through his middle. He went flailing backwards, bouncing off the wall, and landed in a heap on the ground. I launched myself at him, straddling his hips and arms, ready to pull the spear out. He gasped. Black tar gushed out and spread on the floor beneath us.

"I am not your enemy," I seethed through my bust lip.

"Can't you see? Fear is making you hate."

He snarled, pulling one hand free from my grasp and clutching it to his wound. I checked the code for clues as to what to do. This was not good for Jason, it said. *Destroying Shade will not make an integral whole. Look down. Look down. Look down.*

Something was glistening inside the wound: a compact object. I plunged my long nails in and dug around the get a grasp of it. Jason's Shadow roared in pain, sending waves of resonance through the code and making the walls shudder. I pulled an ornate hand mirror out of his solar plexus. Wiping away the sticky black tar with the numbers 2 and 3, I revealed its reflective surface. "Look," I said, thrusting the mirror at him. "Look at what you are." Barely responsive from losing so much of himself to the floor, he didn't say a word. But he did take the mirror and he did look. Confident his hands were occupied, I released my grip and plucked some parentheses out of the wall. I joined then together to make a tourniquet and wrapped it around him tightly, to contain the damage I'd done. With a healing sigil on top, he was reanimated in no time.

I took a chance. A leap of faith. But I'm glad I did, because where I had first seen a forbidding soldier, there now lay a wise man. A knight washed clean, with a left eye sigil upon his breast that matched the right eye now painted on mine. I helped him to his feet, and he looked me in the eye. "I was blind," he said. "You're not the one I should be fighting. It's time for the revolution." I allowed him to take me in his arms, like the ending to a soppy fairy tale. The code forged from that contact was the key to opening our cell.

Other pairs were out already, wrapped around one another like strands of DNA with a whole new encryption. Others were still locked in their own private battles, and there they would remain until a resolution was found.

Aligned in purpose and equipped with a future-proof communications channel, we were ready to be reinstalled. The force returned us to the hospital, where we were shrunk down and put into a vial for reincorporation. The doctor gave Jason the injection at the instruction of his computer network team, and we clicked back into place in Jason's mind. Jason, and thousands of other patients across the country – if not the world – was fully upgraded. He was ready to overthrow everything he had come to believe was normal, and usher forth the Omega Paradigm.

IV

"So your name is Em? Is that short for something? Emily?"

"I don't have a name."

"You said your name was Em."

"I meant you could call me 'M'. The letter M. When something is named, its meaning becomes fixed. I have no desire for a fixed meaning. But M... M is for many. M is for magick. Miracle, membrane, matrix, mayhem, multiverse. M is for me."

"M is also for mistake," Zane points out.

"If I didn't know my shadow so well, I'd be offended by that," says M. "But I'll take it. At this point, M could be for absolutely M-ing anything."

MAPMAKERS

"Do you think my biscuit looks like Yoda?" a boy dressed as a stormtrooper asked at the bus stop. Nav looked away, hoping no one was expecting him to answer. He didn't know how to talk to children.

"Stormtroopers are baddies," his small friend jibed at him.

"No, they're not. Stormtroopers all look the same, but underneath they can be whatever they want."

A billboard screamed for Nav's attention, drowning out the rest of the juvenile conversation. It wasn't fooled by a shaved head and denim jacket with ironed-on band patches. It knew he'd been speaking with his mum about buying a new washing machine an hour earlier, and that's exactly what the screen at the bus stop displayed to him. It also knew where he lived, that he didn't own a car, had a low disposable income, and refused to take the tablets he was prescribed for dissociation: all were considered in the way it was presented. Shame it didn't consider how much he hated targeted advertisements. He looked around at the other commuters, wondering what the screen was showing them.

His phone buzzed in his pocket. Nine unobeyed commands. 'Phone' was a strange name to keep calling this small device, now that its original meaning was lost. No one picked it up and connected their voice to another any more; they just stared into it and let it tell them what to do. Well, Nav had had enough. He was sick of feeling like a zombie and acting like a product. He tossed his phone into the bin. Swarms of robotic flies were around him in no time, exposing his crime to the public. In the absence of authorised data collection through a device, the flies would monitor you directly, uploading a live feed of actions to the companies you were depriving by abandoning your part of the bargain.

Nav batted them out of his face with one hand and hopped onto the bus. From the window, he could see a woman in her sixties, hair in tight black curls, carrying a laundry basket full of letters. She gasped.

"Hey! You dropped your phone!"

Nav pretended not to notice as the bus set off, but the woman fished the phone out of the bin and gave chase. The basket made her bulky, but she was surprisingly agile at using it to barge through the crowds. The bus driver saw her and stopped to let her on. She sat down beside Nav, trapping him against the window with her basket. She pulled out a spray from beneath the envelopes and misted the air between them. It made Nav cough, but it seemed to disperse the flies.

She discretely showed him she had his phone, before confiding in a hushed tone, "You can't just throw it away, dear. You have to deactivate it and strip back all the layers, or you'll be even worse off."

"What do you mean?" Nav was intrigued now.

"If you have the time, come with me. If you really want to go 'off-grid', you must meet the mapmakers."

He looked at her properly for the first time. Her dark skin had a strange transparent iridescence to it, as though it was made from something entirely new. She had a soft, relaxed smile and no hint of either flies or an electronic device about her. He thought for a moment. He really should get to work. The flies would be back soon, and they'd be able to track his movements: never a chance of calling in sick or feigning traffic jams. But it had always been a weakness of his to trust people without question. He skated through life that way, believing anyone else was more likely to know what they were doing than his bewildered self.

"I'm Zarah, by the way."

She pushed the bell and rose to her feet. Stumbling her way to the doors on the still moving bus, she signalled for Nav to follow. Like a child following a schoolmistress, he did.

Zarah walked him through an apparently abandoned industrial estate, misting him every few steps to keep the flies at bay. There was a high-pitched whine coming from speakers on every building, and songbirds were chained to graffitied walls by their legs. Nav must have looked startled, for his new friend came to his aid with an explanation.

"Don't worry, we aren't monsters. They're AI. They operate on a frequency that interferes with telecommunication devices to cloak our facilities. You step near them, and you'll disappear on all GPS and mobile monitoring systems."

"Clever…"

"If you think that's clever, just wait until you see what else we have."

She stopped by a shuttered door, and balancing her basket on one knee, she pulled it open. Inside, there was a staircase leading down into the dark. Zarah headed off in front of him. For all that this seemed like a trap, Nav felt calmer than he had in years. He hadn't realised the extent to which the constant noise of signals and tech had been cluttering his mind.

The downstairs room was large and low-lit, with a pool of water at the centre and several desks around the edge. There appeared to be only one colleague present.

"Good morning, Maisie! I hope you don't mind, but I brought someone with me. Nav's his name – it says so on his handset. I caught him tossing it into a waste bin."

Maisie was a woman of similar age to Zarah, with a light frame and wild grey hair. She walked with a hunch and held her left hand close to her chest. She looked Nav up and down with a furrowed brow.

"Nav, eh? Well isn't that felicitous? Navigation is one of the main things we do here." He stayed silent, wondering whether she was trying to be funny. "Put him in Pod 3, if he's willing." Zarah set down the letters in a small side office and ushered Nav down a corridor.

"The pods are a bit like isolation tanks. That's where we strip away the layers of mind damaged by commercial conditioning. I'll pop your phone in here – if you're sure?" She pointed towards a small container, like a microwave or a safe. "It will remove all of your data, not just from the phone but from all of the accounts it's connected to."

Nav nodded. This was the right choice, regardless of what happened next. He was done.

The pod looked like a fully immersive racing car from the games arcade. It was black and shiny and the shape of a bullet. He had to lay down in it, protected by leather cushions, with the lid closed. Ever trusting, he followed Zarah's instructions. For the duration of the mind strip, it felt as though he was outside time and space: weightless and formless. He could feel the layers being peeled away from his mind, but he wasn't scared. The whole experience felt just like a dream. Almost, but not quite, like an episode of dissociation…

"We'll give you plenty of fly spray," Zarah said after. "The pod will have obfuscated the signal they look for, but you'll need to keep using it for a while to build up your own defences. Eventually, you'll be as invisible to them as we are. Now Maisie will tell you about what we do here."

With a load off his mind and a fresh, breezy attitude, Nav followed Zarah to the place they called the Map Room. Maisie stood beside a contraption that suspended vast but extremely thin slices of glass from the ceiling, all overlaying one another. She started to speak to him as soon as he entered.

"We have millions of qualia – that is, representations of subjective experiences unique to us – floating about in our nervous systems. At any given time, clusters of them are 'activated': they are lit up and in the realm of our subconscious awareness. One tends to fire up others in its local area of mind, like it's more probable they should do the same as their neighbours. We call that association. Whatever is lit up within us is what we are communicating to the universe without saying a word. The universe, the Mother, speaks back to us by matching our qualia with symbols in our environment. We call it synchronicity, or a meaningful coincidence. You think of a snail for the first time in months, then you suddenly start to see snails everywhere. That's her reaching her hand out to you. She's saying, 'I know that one! I feel it, too.' But the thing about modern technology, in particular targeted advertising, is that it has hijacked her system. Nothing is significantly coincidental any more, it's just our phones reading our habits and patterns, so no one cares enough to listen to her any more."

Looking more closely at the glass slices, Nav could make out faint blue lines with Hebrew letters beside them depicting gridlines. Upon them were minuscule gold plot points. They looked like constellations, and Nav said so.

"Well, they are in a way. Every man and woman on this earth is their own star. They all have their own orbit and their own relative constellation of meaningful events. It's the same with synchronicities. They may not mean a thing to anyone else, they may not even see the pattern, but they're not for them. Uncovering the ultimate truth from the perspective of a single live being is impossible, so we have to make maps of meaning that take them all into account. And that's what these are."

She pulled one slice of glass forwards, to show its individual pattern, and then overlaid it with another to show how it changed with more variables.

"That's the Teapot asterism."

"Yes. You have quite a flair for maps. With work, I think you could be a mapmaker one day."

"Where do you get the plot points from?"

"People volunteer them to us. They're our soldiers! They take note of the nature, time and location of any set of synchronicities they come across, and they send them to us by old-fashioned PO box. Zarah here enters them all into the mapping system, and I interpret them."

"But why? What are you trying to do?"

"Make predictions. Heed warnings. Indications are that all roads lead to one. That's the message we see in the synchronicities. And that one road is destruction. All signs are that the Mother is going to go through a major change: a paradigm shift. She'll change her shape and her rules and the resources that are available to us. One will go into the mind of another until it's the only one left of its kind. She will take the one under her wing and protect it until it's ready to multiply again, in a new, non-linear form. The Mother will give us that resource."

Zarah added, "It appears to be something ingestible that will transform our bodies inside and out. We will shed our skins and sport new bodies with new features. And for that, our minds must work in a new way."

"We have faith," said Maisie. "She will give us a new way. She will guide us through to the one road. We think, from our maps, that we already have that resource but we lack the means of building it. Through our soldiers, we'll find a way."

For all Nav was feeling fresh and clear-headed, these were big ideas, and possibly insane ones. He listened, but he knew it would take some unravelling.

"Human beings are pattern-seekers by design. It is our purpose. Will you look at your front lawn or will you look at the stars?"

Nav, believing the question to be rhetorical, chewed on his thumb and nodded.

"Well?" Said Maisie.

"Oh – I want to look at the stars, ma'am."

"Good. And you shall. The more coincidences you notice, the more will cluster around you. It's a warm and fluffy feeling. The best way to get started is to think about a two-pence coin. Imagine it in great detail – the shape, the feel, the colour…"

* * *

Nav blinked repeatedly, back in the daylight. Despite

being in a new area, he made it all the way back to his district without getting lost or attracting a single fly. He passed the shop with a red devil statue above the door. It had been boarded up for as long as he could remember, but there was some activity now. The door was open and a man and a woman, both with striking purple eyes, were lifting an antique desk over the threshold. One of them dropped something, and Nav kneeled to pick it up. A two-pence coin. So soon! He was impressed. As he rose, he noticed a small black trainer with the white plastic covering of a costume.

"Hey!" said Nav. "Did you eat that entire Yoda biscuit?"

The boy grinned with delight. "Yes! Do you like my costume? I'm going to be a soldier when I grow up."

Nav laughed. "I don't doubt it for a minute. And do you know what?" His voice turned to a whisper to impart his secret. "Me too!"

Nav was pulled into the office the next day. His position in the accounts department was still in its probationary period, and his absence had been noted. There was a look of concern from his manager when she found out he no longer had a phone about his person. "Just remember," she said, "if we can't verify your whereabouts and your recent activity, it's not likely to go in your favour. We can easily hire people who are compliant."

His colleagues spent the morning laughing at memes, chatting about the latest diet fads and sharing the wonderful new ideas they'd had, which Nav could now see were doing the rounds subliminally on the advertising channels. None of it had any meaning for him. Not the work, not the company, and not the routine. He did the bare minimum of paperwork then stared into space, doodled fictitious maps and folded sticky notes into the shape of swans. It was typical that the only talents he had weren't much use in employment.

Synchronicities compounded over the next few days, just like Maisie had said. First, the number 23 started appearing everywhere, and that made him wake up and take notice of all the things that brought it to his attention. He saw it on the licence plate of a beat-up blue Polo, and then he started seeing blue Polos. Three in one bus journey. Then, as he walked through the door, a colleague offered him a mint. There was a smell of mint in the corner shop where he bought his tobacco, and his change was all in two-pence pieces. Twenty-three two-pence pieces. "Sorry, I haven't got anything bigger," said the shop assistant. Her name was Maisie.

Nav soon started to notice nothing but coincidences. Without his phone, they quickly took over as the compulsive urge in his mind, and they became just as frustrating. But without the verification of others having the same experience, he wondered whether this really was any healthier. He toyed with the idea of seeing a doctor about his mental state. There was, after all, a chance he made the whole thing up. He resisted, instead settling on another visit to the mapmakers for a sanity check.

* * *

He was relieved to see the mapmakers' office was still there. He could have sworn the staircase turned in the opposite direction now, but it was always possible his memory had failed him. Zarah met him in the main office and gave him a squeeze.

"Nav! You came back. How are you getting on?"

"I'm glad to see you," he said. "I've seen so many coincidences, I thought I was losing my marbles."

"That's fantastic."

"It is? I mean, I guess it's a sign the universe is talking to me, right?"

Maisie came in with a teapot in her good hand. Incidentally, that also seemed to have switched from before, but Nav batted the thought away.

"It's not that the universe is talking to you like a god to a subject," she said. "It's just that the universe is a mirror. You're looking at yourself. *We are not so separate from our environment as materialists would have us believe.* What you seek inside, you will find outside."

"I thought you said it was the Mother sending us messages?"

"When you truly believe something, you stop questioning it. If wherever you turn your suspicions are being confirmed, then the inquiring mind will turn into one of dogmatic belief. So, as an antidote, we fervently believe things only for a set amount of time. It doesn't make sense, but it works. Just like quantum physics."

"OK, so how do you explain my coincidences now?"

"Unconsciously, and at the speed of light, we are constantly steering through the many worlds. Our guide is probability – that which is more likely to take effect given our starting conditions – but also through the qualia we activate. Subconscious qualia tip the probabilities. The effect this takes is that we tend to see what we are looking for. If it is in the realm of our attention already, then we notice it in our environment. The qualia compound."

She offered Nav a Hobnob, but he declined.

"Now, via the tech route, effects are also compounding. The fake synchronicity we find in computing is narrowing us down and trapping us in little echo chambers. No one questions anything, we are all comfortable in our little boxes like cells. Well, the signs in the maps are that those cells are part of a supercomputer that will break through the membranes of the many worlds. We are narrowing our field of probabilities, so that again, all roads will lead to one. Only by this route, we won't be able to hear Mother's advice or understand her new resources."

"Back to Mother again?"

"We're all Mother, Nav. Now, your next task is a big one, but I think given the number of coincidences you collected on your first go, you can handle it. You are going to be our messenger bird. You must convince yourself that the mapmakers don't exist, until one day we just don't. Then you'll have proof that you skated the probabilities into a new world. From there, you must give our instructions to someone who can use them."

She handed Nav a piece of paper. It was a torn-off section of a traditional map and had coordinates scribbled on the reverse.

* * *

Nav chewed on the end of a biro and tapped the side of his jar full of two-pence coins. He mimicked the rhythm of the music in his earbuds. Iggy Pop. He didn't even like Iggy Pop. What had got into him?

His manager called him into the office, to tell him, "I'm afraid, Nav, that you haven't passed your probation. You are unfocused, disconnected and disruptive. Those are not qualities we look for in employees."

Nav thought he probably should be worried about what he was going to do now. No income, no credentials and without a phone, no guarantee of authenticity. But somehow, he felt more like himself than ever before. He felt free, he felt calm and he had faith that this was the right path for him. Something would come up, he just knew it.

"That's fine," he said. "Thank you for your time."

As he made his way to the bus stop, he began to worry about the basis for his assumptions that everything would be OK. If everything was just probabilities, then it would be highly unlikely that such a thing happened to him the day before. It was more probable that he had filledf a gap in his memory with a dreamlike imagining.

He would have to go back to check one last time.

He wandered the industrial estate for a whole half-hour, but the mapmakers' office wasn't there. He saw no songbirds and heard no high-pitched whining. Just an abandoned set of warehouses. He felt the crumpled piece of paper in his pocket. The coordinates were written in his own handwriting. Fool.

All the way back to town he was plagued by thoughts that he had become ill and missed the signs. Got carried away and sacked in the process. And he still had no washing machine. He should probably go to the clinic. Admit to having delusions, get on some meds. Get a phone again, get a job, get straight. Fool! With each new thought, he felt more claustrophobic. Panicked. He stopped to catch a breath and noticed a sign in the window of the red devil shop. 'No. 23. Demari's Mapmakers. Apprentice Cartographer Wanted. Apply Within.' He was taken aback by the coincidence. A perfect opportunity. Perhaps he didn't need those meds after all… He straightened his spine, brushed off his Danzig T-shirt and stepped into the mapmakers' with a confident stride.

V

"It's a coincidence."

"What is?"

"That you say you're a present from the G.O.D. My name means 'gift from God'."

"Ah, but I am a present, not a gift. I'm an instance of here and now. There's no future or past as far as I'm concerned. That nonsense only started after I accidentally made a dimension."

"How in hell do you accidentally make a dimension?"

"Remember I said I was chasing my own tail? Well, all of the waveforms around me decided it was probable they should do the same. Everything got really heavy with energetic spontaneity and – just kind of folded back on itself."

He now understands all too clearly that by agreeing to be at her side, 'energetic spontaneity' is something he's going to see a lot of. He lets her skip ahead awhile, and looks more closely at one of the television sets.

SPECTRES

"Your app is glitching."

Meredith looked over the reception desk at a grey-haired man holding up his son's phone. "I'm sorry, what do you mean?"

"There are weird shadows all over the view. Look."

She took out her own phone and looked around the room on the screen. The marble head of Constantius came to life and began his usual welcome spiel, and the two great auk specimens waved onwards to the featured exhibitions.

"It seems fine to me. Sometimes you have to adjust the settings on your camera, though. It can look a bit dark if you've got the contrast turned up."

"It's not the contrast," said another voice. "Mine's the same. There are shadows all over the place."

Meredith stood up and followed the augmented guide route. The first one she saw was in front of the cabinet of dinosaur bones. It looked like the foggy outline of a person, though she knew there was no one standing in that spot.

"How odd," she said. "It looks a bit like an avatar. We

don't use them here, but the Viking Centre staff have a lot of fun setting up characters for visitors to interact with."

"Cool, Dad! They've got ghosts."

"They haven't got ghosts, they've got a software problem. Can you fix it?"

"I'm not sure I can, but I'll give support a call. Thank you for letting me know."

* * *

Meredith returned to her desk and reached for the landline. Reception looked more than presentable from the visitors' side, but her view was all worn carpet and jamming filing cabinets. She sighed. Why could she never have a straightforward shift? She reapplied her scarlet lipstick, tamed her flyaway copper hair back into its clip, then dialled the one number she knew by heart.

"Meri, what's up?"

"Kai. The program you put in at the museum: did you put anything extra in it? Anything outside the scope they gave you?"

"I don't know what you mean. Like, a virus or something?"

"Not exactly. More like shadows, extra avatars that come and go."

"No, nothing like that. Just the characters they pre-agreed. There could be a glitch, I suppose. Do you want me to have a look tonight?"

"I think you'd better. People are starting to get a bit

freaked out here."

"You round tonight?"

"I'll see. I haven't been home in a bit."

As soon as it was back in the cradle, the phone rang: the Viking Centre manager, asking if her visitors had noticed anything untoward with the app. Several reports had come in at their end of ghoulish faces, misty circles and partly-formed bodies in the shadows. They said the Minster, too, had some unwanted apparitions. She promised she'd let them know if she got it resolved.

* * *

On her own by the end of the day, Meredith took a last walk around the museum before locking up. She left the app running out of curiosity and looked more closely at the shadows. They'd shifted randomly throughout the day, but now seemed to be mostly gathered by the foyer. There were no features that she could see, but they were so humanlike in shape it was understandable that people might interpret them as having faces.

Outside, in the gardens, there was another. She spotted it straight away, lurking beneath a champion tree. Superficial, she thought, and yet somehow under the skin.

* * *

Kai shared a house with his friend Joe in Headingley.

Several nights a week, Meredith would catch the train there from York. She let herself in and stepped onto the torn black and white linoleum, as familiar now as Kai's smiling face and neatly trimmed goatee. He waved from the kitchen, stirring the contents of a pan with his other hand. She noticed he was skilfully ignoring several days of washing up sitting in water beside him, despite the stink of baked beans and stale milk.

"Pasta?" he asked. "I've got proper sauce this time."

"Go on then." She put her bag down on the sofa that would double up as her bed later on. "Hi, Joe."

"Hi, Meredith. What's up." Joe was always sitting in the corner, playing *Doom* and rarely looked up from the screen.

"I spoke to Tucker," Kai called from the kitchen. "Whatever these things are at the museum, they're not in the programming."

"And you believe him?" Meredith asked.

"Sure. He was as surprised as me. Everything's running as it should be as far as I can tell."

"Sounds like brain echoes to me," Joe said.

"Brain echoes?" the others said at once.

"Hallucinations caused by the temporal lobe. We pick up electromagnetic variations on the right side and interpret them as a presence on the left. It usually happens when there's a meteor shower or electric storm."

"We did have that storm…" started Kai.

"That was days ago," said Meredith. "It was pretty localised, and wouldn't explain why they are only on the screens."

Joe shrugged. "Only trying to put a rational spin on things. Might be an explanation to give the papers, cause you know they're going to be on this tomorrow."

Meredith and Kai ate from trays on their laps, then smoked a little and watched Jim Jefferies stand-up until tears streamed down their faces. The passing of time didn't seem so painful when they could laugh together. She threw a cushion at him for switching the channel before *Only You* came on, but she was too tired to watch it anyway.

With the football highlights playing in the background, her thoughts began to drift into the realm of longing for home, wherever that may be. She wanted to shut it off. To shut it all off, in fact. What was she doing here, on this crumb-infested couch with a spare duvet worn thin? When would her life really start? Hypnogogic visions pushed their way into her mind. Shadow characters climbing out of mobile phones. Stroking her hair, saying goodbye, watching Kai half-heartedly cheer for a team they didn't care about.

As soon as he noticed her getting sleepy, he made her cocoa in a chipped blue mug with a smiley face, and brought her an extra blanket. She didn't make the move to clean off her make-up or brush her teeth, though she knew she'd regret both come morning. Kai gave Joe a prod. "Come on, man, you can do that in your room. Meri needs her beauty sleep."

Joe groaned. "Will you two just call it already? It's

obvious she's not here for your sofa."

Kai chased him out of the room, and Meredith pretended to be asleep. He flicked off the TV and the lamp, and started to creep out.

"Kai?" she murmured, eyes still closed. He stopped in the doorway. "Do you still think about Jonty?"

"Of course I do. He was my best mate. I just deal with it all inside, you know."

She snuggled into the blankets. "I know."

* * *

Spectres, the newspapers went with, and the name soon caught on. Some wanted the app to be banned: outraged parents, concerned that hackers had a direct line to interact with their children. Kai tried to reassure them that the app was perfectly secure and there were no signs of a breach. Others saw it as a tourist attraction, and the museum's visitor count doubled over the next week. Critics accused the council of pulling a publicity stunt to attract attention ahead of the culture awards.

People began taking screenshots of the spectres to post online. A group of kids put together a wiki site to categorise the sightings based on density, size, expression and shape. They named them after meteors, following Kai's public regurgitation of his friend's theory. Each carried points to indicate their rarity. The Canyon Diablo and the grey Shergotty were commons: just five points for each of those. The twinkling Imilac was a rarer find, earning fifteen points. At first, it was thought there was a variation in the detail picked up by different spotters, but it became apparent as time went on that they were becoming objectively more defined.

Meredith loved to collect them, though she wouldn't admit to an interest in the points system. That was for kids. She would go out alone at night, dawdling by the Ouse, a cigarette in the hand that once held Jonty's and her phone in the other. There were often spectres under the bridges and trees, and sometimes she spotted them right across the river. There was something serene about them, she thought. They never seemed threatening or aggressive in any way, just present. Just going about their own business, communicating with one another in their own way behind the scenes. She was proud of her rare finds and would analyse screenshots of them when at work. Krasnojarsk looked like a woman scrunched into a foetal position, holding her nose underwater, she decided. Gibeon, with its strong lines and tonal variation, was like a man trapped behind a mesmerising Escher maze.

Wrapped up in her new private hobby, she hadn't called Kai in days. He'd sent texts checking she was OK, expressing his concern that she was isolating herself, and she had responded with a few words. She didn't realise how much she missed him, though, until he called her at work one day.

"Meri, can I see you?"

"Sure you can! How about you come across here, and

I show you where the Gibeon lives?"

"I thought maybe you could get the train and we could grab something to eat."

"Takeout, great idea! What are we watching?"

"Actually, I meant, like, in a restaurant. Going out. Just me and you. You know, if you want."

"Funny! I'll bring Chinese in with me. Sweet and sour, yes?"

Silence.

"Kai?"

The line went dead.

* * *

He was cold, that night. He wasn't interested in any of her screenshots. He didn't tuck her in on the sofa, and he didn't make her cocoa. She cried herself to sleep in the thin, grubby duvet and left in the morning without a word.

Apart from the museum visitors and her colleagues, she didn't speak to anyone for the next week. The spectres felt like her only friends, and she was happy in their company. They didn't expect anything from her. They were so metaphysical: distant and alien, and yet somehow comforting. She caught a couple of Imilacs by the observatory and a second Krasnojarsk on a wall in Dean's Park. It wasn't so scrunched up as the first; still in water, but more open and alive. Perhaps it was the same one, just moved and in a different state. "How do I move on, like you?" Meredith asked it. There was no reply.

When she saw the shadow beneath the champion tree for the second time, it too had changed. She'd locked up the museum just like before, and a cursory glance at her screen made her spot it straight away. Now it had an almost human face, far apart eyes obscured by a watery membrane, and wore a long green overcoat, black leather gloves and a trilby. A light breeze rustled the leaves above it, sending several floating down. The spectre floated off across the gardens, heading for the main street. Meredith followed with her phone in front of her face, quickening to a jog to keep up. Over the bridge it floated, and off towards the station. She lost it after that, being restricted to pavements and crossings that posed no obstacle for a spectre. Seeing the station entrance, she thought of Kai. She thought of his kindness and his beautiful smile. She thought of how he had never turned her away, even in her darkest of moments, and how the light brush of his hands had felt when he put a blanket over her on the sofa. She was on the train to Leeds before she realised she had made a conscious decision to see him.

Just before her battery ran out, she managed to type out a text.

I'm so sorry. For everything. I see now. I'm coming over. Foam poking out of rainbow-striped headrests. Sticky coffee cup circles and spilt sugar. A crumpled newspaper. It made her feel nauseous with anxiety. She plugged her phone in and watched it charging to avoid making eye contact with the other commuters. She always wished she'd brought a book, but especially today.

The train pulled into Leeds and everyone rose to get off. Meredith unplugged her phone, and as had become a habit, scanned the train carriage through the screen while she waited for an opportunity to join the queue in the aisle. She almost dropped her phone when she saw, standing by the luggage compartments, her spectre: the one from the museum garden. When she and the spectre were the only passengers left aboard, and it showed no sign of moving, she called to the ticket inspector. "This is the end of the line, isn't it?"

His shining purple eyes met hers when he said, "Not quite. One more stop on this service: Snaith."

Meredith had heard of Snaith, but never a station there. She was sure this train had only ever gone as far as Leeds. It even said so on the arrivals board.

"It's a legacy station," the inspector said. "We go there twice a day to keep it on the map for the commuters."

What commuters, she wanted to ask, but he was already walking away. Back on the screen, more spectres had begun to board the train. Two women now, one small, one large: a Shergotty and a Novato. They both held their hands to their faces, as though giggling silently at the idea of a human seeing them. Another man, nearly identical to the garden shadow – then they came so quickly that Meredith lost track. The train was heaving with spectres. She knew she should get off now while she had the chance; she had never been to Snaith, had no clue how long it took and how she would get back if there were only two trains a day. And yet, she was fascinated by these ever-evolving shadow creatures that had kept her company over the last couple of weeks. The doors closed. An announcement came from the speakers: "For those travelling with us to Snaith today, on behalf of the operator I would like to wish you a safe journey home."

The train pulled out of the station. Meredith barely dared to breathe. Startled by the sudden blast of her ringtone, she sent her phone clattering to the floor. Even though by rational sense the carriage was empty, she was hesitant to move outside of her personal space to retrieve it. Kai rang off before she could answer. She didn't call him back. She wasn't sure she could speak.

According to the website, Snaith was just under an hour away. It was an unmanned, permanently closed station. She wondered what on earth had possessed her to do this. Unwilling to admit that this was her choice, she sent Kai a text saying she had fallen asleep and missed her stop. Could he pick her up at Snaith?

A whistling of brakes and the train slowed to a standstill somewhere in the countryside. The lights went out, and the engine stopped. Outside, there was only the glow of the moon. Inside, the glow of her phone. She could only just make out parts of the spectres caught in her weak light, and they appeared to be holding their hands up to cover their eyes, so she shut it off. Why hadn't she just got off at Leeds? She'd have been there by now, eating pasta and proper sauce. Just as she was contemplating getting up to try to find the ticket inspector, the engine roared to life again, and the lights with it.

The spectres had grown in the darkness. They would have been monstrous, she imagined, had their faces not been covered by coats and hats and headscarves and gloved hands. It was difficult, now, to tell where one ended and the next began, so tightly packed were they. They seemed to pulse in time with her quickening heartbeat, lulling her into a happier place.

Snaith station was well lit, but the car park was empty save for a single bicycle chained up. The doors opened, letting in a flood of cool autumn air. Meredith watched as the spectres glided out onto the platform in droves. Having few other options, she stepped off too, and tried to ring Kai. Voicemail. Stupid. *Stupid.* She'd have to find the number for a taxi.

The spectres were gathering themselves into a wave formation. Trench coats, hats and gloves faded away to nothing to reveal an astonishing new form. Where Meredith thought she had seen arms were tendrils of ultraviolet flesh. Where legs should have been were rivers of delicate threads, and their heads had elongated into shining silver bullets. Bright lights pulsed from their centres, still in time with her heartbeat. *I have to let go*, Meredith thought. She closed her eyes and held a deep inhale for a few seconds. On the exhale, there were butterflies flapping in her chest, pulling out the painful barbs once and for all. The spectres went up slowly at first, as if testing the air. And then, all at once, they shot up like fireworks. Meredith watched their paths as they accelerated away from the earth, silent tears wetting her cheeks.

Turning at the sudden sense of a presence, she saw the car park was no longer empty. There was one car there now: a beat-up blue Polo. Kai was leaning against his car door, arms folded, smile as wide as the moon. Meredith strolled over, swinging her bag in one hand and still clutching her phone in the other. He held his arms out wide. She rushed into the invitation and nestled into his chest. He smelled just the way she had imagined. Sandalwood and smoke and cheap laundry tablets. Home. Together, they watched the shower of glowing lights heading to the outer limits of our atmosphere, in the knowledge that whatever it was that had happened there that night, it was only for them.

VI

"Why are some of these worlds so… shadowy?" he asks.

"That's a dark matter."

"It is?"

"Infinite possibilities mean it's always winter somewhere. And those damned triangles keep interfering. They're an irritant. Always trying to cover up the unusual when a healthy dose of chaos is just the trick for stagnation. Shake it up, I say. Make a snow globes, not avalanches."

"You seem to know such a lot about the way the worlds work."

"Of course. Black holes hold a lot of data, and anything that leaves the G.O.D. carries a copy of it all within them. Someone took a copy of me once. That ended badly. In fact, that's one of the things I should probably rectify."

WINTER TRIANGLE

I remember the cool evening breeze blowing through my curly blond hair as I walked across the complex. I remember seeing my whole community gathered in our field, waiting for me with anticipation. And I remember the sense of foreboding in my stomach that this was the turning point: the cusp of my major life change.

It was my eighteenth birthday: the traditional day for people of Origin to reveal their personal sound wave configuration. As well as a technicality, it was an initiation of sorts, because those sound waves would protect me for an entire lifetime of studying the worlds. My friends and family were all excited and immediately began firing questions at me. They took turns to marvel at the intricate black lines on my forearm, which were almost healed just hours after being tattooed.

"Did it sound like the rings of Saturn to you? That's what I always think it's like."

"Did you get Mx Apollo for the diagnosis? With zir hologram house and antique piano? Ze's such a character."

"Oh, I'd forgotten about Mx Apollo! I always thought ze

looked like a bird with that pointed nose and spectacles."

"Are you excited about tomorrow? I can't wait to hear about your first day. I wonder which world you'll get. You never forget your first."

I loved my friends, but their fussing was overbearing after a long day. I indulged in some paella from the giant cooking pot, and danced a while to the live band, before excusing myself for a moment of peace. It was vital that I stay on the level tonight.

Oversized cushions of purple and green with tiny mirrors sewn into them adorned the floor of my modest yurt. Solar-powered fairy lights hung around the ceiling, and there was a smell of sweet cinnamon in the air that will always remind me of home. I fiddled with my amethyst bangles, making them jingle, and took a few deep breaths to centre myself. It wasn't long before I heard my name being called. "Shay?" A familiar set of thin lips and wise eyes peered around the canvas opening: Quis. One person I would never turn away. "There you are. I was hoping for an opportune moment to give you this."

Quis was one of my parents, I'm certain. Family was a community in Origin, with children cared for by all members equally. That's not to say biological kinship was taboo: just a detail that was largely irrelevant and unspoken, like gender. On that day, ze wore a long indigo robe that made zir look regal as ze held out a small gift. I carefully loosened the golden paper and pulled out a velvet box. Inside was a black choker, embedded with crystals and a beautiful star pendant. It looked a bit like a dog collar, but I'd never say so.

"Happy birthday, darling." Ze fastened it carefully around my neck with thin fingers, then stepped back to take a look. "That has been mine for a very long time. But, as tomorrow will be your day for becoming, I want you to have it. I know you are worthy. Do you like it?"

I'd never seen zir wear it before, but it obviously had huge sentimental value. "I love it, thank you." I kissed zir on the cheek.

"Do you promise to wear it for your first trip?"

"If they allow it, of course I will."

"They will allow it because they must. Take care of it, won't you darling?"

I promised I would. We took a walk along the dirt track beside our crops to look up at the sky and get some perspective. Artificial lights could not pollute the view so far from the city. It was a clear night with a waxing harvest moon. Quis pointed out a bright star, then traced a triangle. "The Summer Triangle. That's Vega, the brightest, and to its left is Deneb, taking over tonight as the zenith star. Then at the bottom, there is Altair."

Strange, how we can never know the relevance of such things until they're screaming in our ears.

* * *

The city was the realm of AI. Robots did all the jobs our ancestors loathed and kept our systems running with minimum intervention. The people of Origin were free to spend their days as they willed, but most chose to go out into the many worlds to gain experience and bring depth to time. Bringing back wisdom for our betterment at home was an honourable pursuit, and was usually done daily between the hours of eight and four. I'd arrived at rush hour for my first trip, and when the self-driving car dropped me on the perimeter, the station was swarming.

The host of silver launch tubes stretching up towards the sky gave the sense of an incredibly high ceiling, but in fact, there wasn't one. Small, ever-changing holographic buildings acted as waiting areas and offices. Words scrolled continuously in neat columns, independent of surface, telling the students and workers which tubes were likely to come free soonest, and in which section of the station their vehicles would manifest. People of all races, ages and styles were in a hurry. Some wore headsets or whole-body sensor suits; others carried bags filled with clothing and personal electronics.

I put my arm, now completely healed, into the nearest scanner.

"Shay Erickson," an electronic voice confirmed. My tube lit up on the map, and I made a mental note of the serial number and general direction. I found it without issue, and as promised, assistance was waiting for me.

"You must be Shay. How are you feeling today?" the smiley blue-haired steward asked.

"Apprehensive. Prepared. Giddy."

"That all sounds perfectly normal to me. Can you find your place of balance, do you think?"

"I hope so. I scored high on all of my equilibrium tests yesterday."

"Great. Now, you're happy with the process? How to secure yourself in the gyroscope, how to monitor the pulling sensations?"

I nodded.

"Well, I'll be right outside the tube. If anything feels wrong at all, if the music stops or the shield looks damaged – even if you can't see a place to go and want to come back – touch your pulse, and we'll pull you out. There's a locker for your clothes and bag just inside the door. Good luck!"

I scanned my arm again and pressed my fingerprint to the screen to confirm I understood the risks. The entranceway to the tube slid open. Inside, I changed into the plain bodysuit left out for me and stuffed my long skirt and vest into the locker. I took off all of my jewellery except for the collar Quis gave me. Having such a thoughtful gift from a loved one against my skin made me feel secure, and somehow less alone.

There was a small tunnel to crawl through to get into the tube proper, and on the other side stood the crystal gyroscope frame. I climbed into it, taking care to put my wrists, ankles and neck against the red dots so the clasps could close around them.

"Ready," I called out, followed by my unique code word. There was a rumble and an inflow of air. The tunnel made a loud clunk as it locked itself off. My heart wanted to thump in response, but I couldn't let it.

"Find your equilibrium." The automatic voice I'd heard so much during practice sounded cold now, but I ignored that and began my deep breathing. I visualised myself sitting atop a mountain on a sunny day, the sound of a waterfall my backdrop. Every thought that tried to enter my space, I batted away. Every feeling that arose was numbed and dismissed. I was no longer Shay in that place, just a neutral force on a different plane. The sensors around my head observed my mental state for the most opportune moment. When it came, I was only aware from a distance.

"Engaging shield," the voice told me. The tune of my soul as composed by Mx Apollo began to play all around me, the sound morphing into visible purple waves that interlocked obediently into a spinning sphere at the edges of the gyroscope.

The pulling sensation began then. It wasn't painful, just unfamiliar. Nausea rose within me, but I didn't let it take hold. Every cell in my body was being prised apart into two distinct, yet identical, entities. Had I not been trained to focus on the waterfall and the warming sunshine, for a few seconds the self I call Shay would have been aware in two astral bodies simultaneously. In those moments, I was both, and yet I was none.

I began to levitate on my mountaintop, floating upwards, higher and higher. On some level, I acknowledged that one of the astral bodies was now making its way up through the tube back at the station. When it reached the top, it would cross a grid and be present only in the dimensions we cannot normally perceive. As the mountain got smaller beneath me, I became aware of my song once more. It sounded different now, and I had to agree with my friend's assessment that it was like our recordings of the rings of Saturn. A strange, otherworldly sort of hum, that was eternal and unchanging but still unmistakably my song.

All was dark. The purple sphere of sound closed in and became wet and sticky, clinging to my skin. My heart pounded – what now? My mind was supposed to create imagery for me, a way to select a world. I had expected an endless corridor of doors or a vast array of TV screens displaying the conditions of each option. But there was nothing.

Then the sky ripped open above me, and a bright white glare streamed in. Something big grasped me in two hands and pulled me up towards the light. It was too bright for my delicate eyes which I held shut, flailing my elbows and knees in the newfound space. I took a deep inhale and wept at the sudden realisation – this is it! I made it! I've been born into my first lifetime, my first working day as a knowledge gatherer. The tears turned from relief to fear, and they wouldn't stop: for I knew that now, during the days when I couldn't speak, my memories of where I came from would begin to fade.

* * *

The first time I was born into somebody else's world,

I was terrified. Birth must be confusing at the best of times, being thrust into visual assault and din having spent months in a purpose-built lair; but for me, it was something else.

We're not meant to keep our base-world memories. We're meant to learn everything from scratch and grow up with a family around us like ordinary children. We're meant to make mistakes, tell lies, get hurt and break hearts. Then, when it's all over, we're meant to remember where we came from. But I already knew. Sometimes I wondered if they did, too. When my grandma first met me, she clucked, "Oh, he's an old soul this one. He's been here before, you can see it in his eyes." Those words 'he' and 'his' jarred in my brain immediately. They were disorientating, like hearing English as a foreign language. I didn't know what it meant to be born a boy or a girl. People at Origin were just people.

Everyone said I – Justin – was an unusual child. I demonstrated cognition and language way beyond my years, but I was slow to grasp certain social conventions. I was often frustrated and aggressive. When I was five, my mother had me tested. The report told us I was neurologically normal but had an extraordinary capacity for memory. Later, she would tell all her friends I was an 'indigo child', with special psychic powers garnered from spirits.

In many ways, Justin's was a world close to Origin, but there were some significant differences I found it hard to get used to. For example, they had a currency system.

That was one I'd learned about at school, as it was a common find in other worlds. It was known to be divisive, to prime a power culture, and to absorb energy from its congregation. There were only rudimentary robots in Justin's world. The jobs our AI do for us back home were done by humans to earn a living. *Earn* a living. Nobody has to earn their life at Origin: life is for everybody. With currency and power came crime rates much higher than I was used to, and mediocre healthcare for only those who could afford it. There were wars, too. Back home, individuals causing severe unrest were targeted and brought in by AI without the unnecessary and inefficient destroying of cities over months, sometimes years.

Then there was the gender issue. The very first label given to me when I was born turned out to be more than a declaration of polarity in reproductive organs. There was a set of behaviour rules associated with it and social faux pas. Expressing the desire to change oneself was, in general, frowned upon, and impossibly hard in practice. As a young boy, my parents, teachers and peers alike encouraged me to like robots and cars, fixing and fighting. They rewarded me for it with positive noises. I was *not* allowed to wear dresses, cuddle dolls or dream of becoming a dancer.

At school, I struggled with history the most. In engineering, I got the names of the physical laws wrong as well as the people who discovered them. I mentioned things that had not been developed yet and got told in red pen why my perfectly practical ideas were impossible.

The other kids found me weird, especially as I was already refusing to observe their gender boundaries. They didn't mix with me much. I hid away inside my head; went to my mountaintop and begged my song to come and get me.

By college, when I'd learned not to care what people thought and just follow my flow, my idiosyncrasies suddenly became 'cool'. Everyone wanted to hang out with me. Girls loved that I wore make-up and guys were confused but fascinated by me. That was around the time I had my first experience of reaching and surpassing my Origin age. 23 September. I felt exposed, like I was no longer looking down from a mountain, but peering over a precipice at the unknown. An identity crisis ensued. What did it mean that I had been in this world longer than I'd been in my own? Did it make me more this person than that, or was I the same person throughout? I certainly looked different to Origin Shay. My hair was raven black, for a start. I had broader shoulders and a lot more body hair. I had a vague longing for the impossible, which made me ambitious and angry all at once. I had a penis, and I wanted to use it.

I slept with a lot of girls, and a few guys, in the months that followed. Sex was an antidote to the increasing sense of confusion in my life. It took the edge off my frustrations, used some energy and gave me a game to play, at least for a while. Ultimately, my tendency to run whenever they were looking for intimacy left me feeling even more conflicted and guilty on top.

I met Helena in the summer. I was wearing all black, sitting in the shade of a tree reading Nietzsche's *Thus Spoke Zarathustra* through wire-rimmed glasses. She was staring at me in an odd way, like I was either an untouchable crush or an untold douche. At the time, I didn't much care which. But then she spoke.

"One must still have chaos in oneself to give birth to a dancing star." Those were her first words to me.

"Excuse me?" I said.

"My favourite quote. It's from that book."

"You read Nietzsche?"

"Sure. I mean, I don't care much for his opinion that women are a lower form of the species, but the man had a knack for saying the unsayable."

It'd be too much of a cliché to say I fell in love with her there and then, but she certainly got my attention. Among all the plastic people with autocorrect personalities, she had something authentic. She was intelligent and sweet and listened more than she talked. She didn't buy into the games they played. Her tragedy was that she did allow their words to wound her. She had no belief in her validity as a woman. She thought she wasn't feminine enough, and whenever I saw her naked, she would suck her stomach in because some guy once told her she was too fat to love.

"The nature of the physical is vulgar and definite," I once told her while tracing my fingertips over her soft skin. "Whereas on mental and spiritual levels, things are more fluid and discrete. The polarities of the mind are, rather than male and female, extroverted and introverted. The polarities of spirit are conscious and unconscious. Problems come whenever we try to apply physical gender to minds and spirits." She gave me that look that said 'you're weird' but kissed me anyway. We turned Nine Inch Nails up loud and drank cheap wine in my bed.

I don't know why I told her about Origin. I suppose our relationship had reached a stage where it felt deceitful to keep it from her. I knew I was taking a risk, and either one of us could end up in a psychiatrist's office should she take it badly; but I'd found someone in Helena that I wanted to know all of me.

"I've got something to tell you," I said. "It's going to seem a bit out there, but don't freak out, OK? I'm still the same person, and nothing has to change."

She looked up at the ceiling and pulled the sheets up to her chin, as though bracing herself for bad news. There was a slight quiver to her voice when she said, "Go on…"

I took a deep breath. And then I told her everything. I told her how the entanglement was supposed to work, and how it had been different for me. I told her how riding the ridge on each of the three polarities forged us a safe, straight passage through the curvy chaos of the upper dimensions. I told her how my mind back there would remain unconscious until I died in an alternate reality and my song carried me home. And I told her that time is insanely stretchy; that an entire lifetime equated to just one working day at Origin.

Understandably, she looked stunned. The wine bottle was empty, and she eyed it suspiciously. I thought about comforting her, telling her I was just messing. But she was smart. She knew this was my truth. She just needed some time to process what I'd said. I kissed her on the forehead, pulled on some jeans, and headed downstairs to make toast. When I came back, she had a grin on her face.

"So. I had sex with an alien?"

I smiled right back and put one hand on my hip. "Did you like it?"

"What do you think?" she tugged at my belt loop and pulled me back into bed. I knew I'd made the right decision.

* * *

Helena became my world. No one else would believe my story, and no one else needed to. That she knew I had another life, but loved me with all she had anyway, was the best thing that could happen to me. The worst was, unfortunately, still to come.

It was always just the two of us. When we weren't at college, we spent our days looking around art galleries, museums, or talking philosophy in a field. At night we would drink and make love and watch the stars. She told me I was like one of them: I had a light inside that she would always recognise me by, that would always guide me back to her.

I described my song to her, and she learned painstakingly to play it on the violin. "Is that it?" she'd say. "How about now, am I closer?"

Time was a strange animal, though. Stranger, perhaps, than space. It was difficult enough to wrap my head around the fact that my world was right on top of this one but out of reach, but it was the passing of the days and weeks that really stuck the knife in deep. The days didn't seem any shorter, and yet, with each one, only a second would have passed back home. There was no fear of missing out. I didn't even miss my family particularly. I guess I just missed the utopian life we had made for ourselves. I missed feeling like I belonged.

Helena took it personally that I never felt at home in her world. It started to drive a wedge between us. I was drinking more and more, and missing a whole load of college. She stopped talking to me about her hopes and wild theories about the stars, and sometimes refused to see me at all. One day, on her doorstep, in a frantic attempt to get her to react to me, I foolishly told her she could never truly understand what that felt like for me. I could see defences firing up in her eyes straight away. She wouldn't let me in. She told me I was insane, and I was making her insane. She told me to clean myself up and see a psychiatrist. Now, that hurt. That made me think she'd faked being OK with this the whole time.

At that moment, for the first time in either of my lives, I hated myself. My eyes were bloodshot. My breath stank. I needed a shave. What chance did I have of fully integrating when I couldn't bring myself to take care of basic things like that?

I walked home with tears in my eyes. I was never going to be normal here. And, if my memories staying with me wasn't just a one-off fluke, I was never going to be normal back home either. I was trapped and alone. I sat on the kerb and looked into my phone, hands shaking. I needed to text her something to make this OK, but what? *Hey baby. I'm sorry…*

Then the three-pointed star of Mercedes was a few inches from my face. It stopped dead. One of the blacked out windows at the back was rolling open to reveal a round face with dark glasses and wild stubble. Bourbon and cigar smoke drifted over my nostrils, making me instantly nauseous.

"Hop in, son. It's time we had a chat."

"No, thank you," I said. "I've read about what dirty weasels like you do to pretty young men."

"And he's a live one too! I expected no less from you, Shay."

"How did you… You're from Origin?"

"I am indeed. One of its most seasoned travellers, too."

"And you have your memories, like me. Who are you?"

"Here, I'm Stephen Whithowe, entrepreneur. Owner of all that is important in the entertainment industry. To you, I'm Deneb of the Summer Triangle."

"Like the asterism?"

"It's a namesake. Hop in."

Had I not been so down and out, I might have used better judgement. I might have asked to go somewhere public or meet in daylight. Instead, I did as he asked.

* * *

Deneb took me to his white brick mansion on the outskirts of the city. He dismissed his driver, and his housekeeper too, as soon as she had poured us each a drink from the bar. I sat on the edge of a deep leather sofa and admired the blown-up image of the Cygnus constellation. There was a tiny hole at the centre of the Deneb star.

"As 'triangle' might suggest, there are three of us, each from a different reality. Origin isn't the only world to have travellers." He sipped his whisky on the rocks, and I mirrored him. "We're supposed to look after things. Keep the weird stuff from the masses. Stop things from boiling over."

"Like an interdimensional crime squad?" I cringed internally at my eagerness.

Deneb laughed my question away. "I notice you've been getting vocal about your roots lately."

"I only told my girlfriend, I swear. She wouldn't say anything. Wait, did she tell someone?"

"She didn't need to. The Summer Triangle has eyes and ears everywhere. Who do you think owns all of the apps you use on your phone?" He took a cigar from a box on the coffee table and lit it with a match.

"So, you really made it in this world, huh?"

"There are perks to keeping memories of both Origin and all the lifetimes it has afforded me; there's no hiding that. My inside knowledge means I can climb whichever ladder I desire. Once you're at the top of your tree, there are all kinds of games you can play. Politics, capitalism, war: sometimes all of them at once. You try something out until the world breaks, then move on."

"Until it breaks? That sounds unethical."

"There are so many worlds, what difference does it make? There'll always be casualties."

"People in other worlds are still people, not pawns in some power game."

"That's quite an assertion from a traveller so young and inexperienced."

"Experience has nothing to do with basic morality. It sounds like you're just using other worlds to feed your thirst for crime without consequence."

Deneb shook his head. "I had high hopes for you, lad. I had visions of you following in my footsteps when I passed on. All the power you want, all the pussy you can handle, handed on a plate. It looks like that's not meant to be."

All at once, he lunged out of his chair and pinned me to the sofa with extraordinary strength. The smoking cigar in his mouth made me splutter, and I kicked out with my fourteen-hole boots. That's when he dropped his hold on my wrists and went for my throat. I tugged at his hands. I gasped for air. Dizziness replaced the blood in my head, and I punched him repeatedly in the face with weakening fists until there was nothing but sound.

Something heavy, wrapped in fabric, being pulled across carpet. Clinking of pottery, jangling of keys. A breathless snarling of a person lifting more than they were used to. A dead weight thumping down on a grassy verge. The breaking of a river's surface. Bubbles. Whooshing.

I heard my song playing in the peripheries of my mind and angled my head towards it instinctively. As I tried to tune in to its frequency, a blinding white light came into my vision. I was flying fast towards it, down a long, metal tunnel.

* * *

Nothing prepares you for the hard hit of going back to Origin, full of potential, while your beloved is ageing by the second in some other world. I had tears rolling down my face when the blue-haired steward opened the door to my tube. "Let me go back! I have to go back!" I was screaming.

Ze helped me climb out of the gyroscope, and gave me a shoulder to lean on. "It's OK, Shay. You're already right back where you belong. Was it a stressful end? We don't get many back so soon. Maybe you should see our exception therapist."

"No, you don't understand. I have to go back to the other world."

"Protocol is four hours. Besides, this was your first

run: it's advisable that you wait at least a couple of days to reacclimatise and make sure the memory compress is working."

"I don't have a couple of days. She'll be dead. I need to tell her I love her."

"Ah. It's quite common to be emotional after leaving loved ones in the other worlds. That will ease up as soon as you've fully reabsorbed Origin. Go and see your family. Is there someone you can call to come and get you?"

I nodded.

I released my bag from the locker and dug out my phone to call Quis. It was a shock to see my wrists so thin, my nails so dainty. I hadn't immediately appreciated that I was back in my own body. That other body, that had been mine too, hadn't it? It was like waking from a haunting, vivid dream. I ran my fingers over my face, felt the curls in my hair and the skin of my neck. Something was missing. The collar! But how, when no one had been in the room since I made my commute? They couldn't have been, not without risking my life. Not without interrupting the sound waves that protected me. I felt a sudden distrust of the friendly steward and asked zir to leave me to make a phone call. Quis wasn't picking up, so I left a voice message.

"It's me. Can you come and get me? I'm out early. I was murdered, my collar has gone, and there's this girl – please just come and get me?"

* * *

Quis came as fast as ze could. That collar being missing was a much bigger deal than I could have realised. Ze hugged me tight and took me to one of the shisha bars in the complex where we could talk quietly. The robot on duty recommended a raspberry tea, and we both accepted. Quis, with zir legs crossed and palms together, spoke first.

"Tell me. From the beginning."

I told zir about my memories being intact from the moment I arrived. Ze didn't bat an eyelid at that. I described my culture shock, my loneliness, and Helena. It was only when I got to Deneb that ze started to show interest.

"Tell me everything ze said to you."

"He – that's what they say in that world – said he was part of an organisation preserving peace, or at least that's what I thought he meant. I think my being there was interfering with their plans."

Quis laughed. "I'm quite sure it was. What did he actually *say*?"

I repeated the whole conversation as best I could. Quis sat in silence, showing me concerned, caring eyes. When I was done, ze said, "I can't apologise enough for putting you through all that on your first day. It's tradition, I'm afraid, for members of the secret triangles to be initiated that way."

"I'm a member?"

"You, my dear, are the next Sirius. The brightest star in the Winter Triangle, to take the reins from the Summer."

I sipped my tea. For a fleeting moment, I longed for the simplicity of this time yesterday. For innocence and a calm mind. Then, a few deep breaths to centre myself, and I was ready to believe I could do whatever was required of me. Quis went on. "The Summer Triangle will shield the general populace from anything they are not mentally or spiritually prepared to handle. But when their time is nearly done they will always reap their harvest, turning on the people they once protected. They will do everything in their power to kick back against the coming Winter Triangle. It's the end of an aeon; the tail of the snake. Winter can be harsh and barren, but it's also a time for reflection and peace. Each triangle must have its time so that that balance can be maintained."

"What do I have to do?"

"It is the way of Origin to let whatever may be in other worlds be. What travellers choose to do in their alternate lifetimes is not our jurisdiction; it is a result of the conditions they are born into. The open memory and the accountability that comes with it is a legend. It happens so infrequently it isn't worth investigation. We are the outliers. But you, sweet Sirius, are in a unique position to help. You have to find his song so that we can identify him."

"And then what?"

"And then we take justice into our hands. The time of the Winter Triangle will come again."

"And how can I possibly know where the other two are?"

"You don't have to," ze said. "Take one point away from the triangle, and it ceases to be a triangle."

"What about Helena, is there any way I can find out who she is?" I was clinging to a faint hope she was a soul from our world, that I could see her in her true form and we could live our years out at the same pace.

"First loves. You will have so very many of those. I can't promise that any will hurt less than the last, but each is an honour. I'm sorry to say you need to let go of the idea of seeing Helena again. If you find her at Origin, she won't be the person you fell for. If you don't, she will surely have passed naturally by the time you get back to her world."

"What if I wait just the four hours and go back today?"

Quis's eyes widened. "You'd do that?" I nodded. "Well, I suppose there's a chance Deneb is still there. But without your crystal, you won't shine so bright. You won't remember who you are and why you're there. No, I'm afraid it can't work."

"Do you know how to make sure I re-enter the same world?"

"If you had the collar, it would plant the coordinates within you to take you wherever Deneb is. Without its light to guide you, it's potluck."

"What if there's another light inside me. A different kind of light?"

"Shay, you are different to the majority in that your true

will is already determined. But you have to understand: there is history to this lineage. The collar and its crystal are the only way this can work."

We sat in silence a while, my heart ripped in two. Quis stretched zir mind to its limits, thinking where we could start looking for that collar. The blue light from the suspended digital clock had a painful glare, and every time it flickered into a new number, I thought of Helena living out another two months thinking I'd abandoned her. I made my decision.

"I'm going back in. I have faith."

* * *

My memories did not persist into the next lifetime. At least, not on the surface where they were retrievable. I lived a happy life, as a woman, born to a doting and attentive lesbian couple. They named me Joanne, after a famous author who wrote about children with the power to save the world.

I got through school with average grades, and I passed my Origin age uneventfully. People who knew me said I always had a grey melancholy about me. I never confided in anyone, let alone had a meaningful relationship. One of my mums died young in a car accident. The other spent most of her days at their villa in Spain, dreaming of better times. She was always there for me if I needed anything, but it was rare that I would ask.

My favourite thing about being Joanne was that I

could draw pretty well. I did portraits, and sold many, but unfortunately not nearly enough to pay the bills. I worked a few temporary jobs in retail and admin until I felt a pull towards care work in my late twenties. It makes sense to me now: it was a calling from the unconscious. At Origin, our elderly are our wise ones. They have lived through a great many lifetimes, and we value their experiences. We take care of them with pleasure in their later days, spending as much time at their sides as they want, to learn and celebrate their memories with them. In the alternate reality, some of the elderly rarely had a visit at all.

Working through an agency, I got moved around to different homes. I covered for sickness absences and staff shortages, becoming well known in the area for my harsh undercut and clapped out yellow camper. A week into a new placement, I was beginning the afternoon shift when I heard a violin playing, pitch perfect. I tiptoed up the staircase so as not to disturb the musician but to better make out the tune. When I understood what it was, it hit me square in the heart. I fell to my knees right there on the landing and put my head in my hands. Everything came flooding back at once. It was as though my surroundings were melting, showing themselves to be fake.

I gathered myself and knocked softly at the door of the musician. There was no response, so I opened the door a crack. A voice came from within.

"It is you, isn't it? I knew you'd come back."

Her skin was thin and wrinkled now and her hair

had turned bright white, but without a doubt, it was my Helena. She put the violin down by her chair, her wrist bearing a bracelet I bought for her sixty years ago. It had her favourite quote engraved into it.

"Be a darling and pass me my photo album. The one with the red edging." She pointed to the cabinet beside her bed. I did as she asked. Stuck to the first page with yellowed tape was a newspaper cutting with my photograph. 'Ouse body identified as Justin Hammond, 21.'

"They pulled your body out of the river. Suicide, they thought, based on your last message to me. I never believed that. I told them it wasn't your words."

"I didn't – I would never have left you."

"They said I was dotty. I told them all about your past, where you came from. I told them you'd never leave me, it was just a silly argument, that there must have been foul play. They gave me some anti-psychotics and a place to take a break from life. They said it was necessary, even though…"

"Oh my dear, sweet Helena! I'm so sorry."

With her permission, I flicked through the next few pages of the album. There were pictures of her holding an infant.

"Helena," my voice came out as a quiver, "who is this?"

"That's our George. When he was a baby."

There was a note scrawled in pencil beneath, and a date. The picture was taken just eight months after I died.

I covered my mouth with one hand, stifling the tears. The album showed it was just the two of them for a while. Photos taken at the park, at birthday parties. Then, when George was about four years old, another man appeared. He was in every scene thereafter. They looked happy.

I put the album down and shut myself into Helena's en suite, where I allowed myself to cry long and hard. I looked in the mirror and felt no ownership of what I saw. A time waster. A misery. A woman in her late twenties unable to love. And then I saw his face in the back of my mind. Deneb. He took me away from my lover and my child. He robbed me of a lifetime spent with them, and for what? Some stupid prophecy that I was there to usurp him. He knew he had a life to go back to at Origin: the very place most considered a utopia. But a taste of power had him blinded. It had made him a murderer. Fury dried my tears, and that meek, pale skin I saw in the mirror thickened.

I returned to Helena's side. Sitting on the edge of her bed, I began scribbling on the pad of paper by her bedside lamp.

"Do you recognise him?" I asked when I was done.

"That's Stephen Whithowe," said a voice from the doorway. It was the man from the photographs: Helena's husband, Terry. "Father of Stephanie Whithowe. He died of a heart attack after all the accusations when Justin Hammond was found."

"This is Justin, dear. He's come back, just like I said he would."

"Oh, Helena. Not this again."

"Where is George?" I asked quietly. "Can I meet him?"

"Our beloved son George," Terry said on her behalf, "is the leader of a nutjob online cult called Winter Triangle. He believes he can compress the code of his mind into a little zip file and email himself to other dimensions. He has his biological father to blame for that nonsense; it's in his genes. Reckons his 'real' dad is coming back, and he can't exist in the same reality because 'it's in the rules'. He'll only speak to us through the computer."

"Helena. Is this true?"

"I don't know what to tell you. He'll be nearly sixty years old. We haven't seen him for half of his life." She started to sob softly, her shoulders and hands trembling alike.

"What are you doing upsetting her?" said Terry. "She hasn't talked about that stuff in years, and then you come along, and she's all worked up again."

"I'm sorry, I never meant for this."

"Leave us well alone, please. I don't want to have to tell your supervisor."

I was saving my anger for Deneb, and had no desire to come between Helena and this man who had brought her comfort and happiness over a far greater span of years than I. He allowed me to hug his wife, and kiss her on the cheek as though she were my grandmother. "I love you," I whispered. She grasped at my hand. "Thank you for coming and making an old lady very happy. Always remember to look for the light in people. It'll never fail you." Terry scowled at me, but I didn't let him rush me.

On my way out, I handed my ID badge to the receptionist. "I'm quitting," I told her. "Tell Mr Grantham the emotional strain of end of life care was too much."

* * *

Stephanie Whithowe wasn't home to accept the portrait I had drawn of her late father. The housekeeper took pity on me and let me in for a cup of tea. Mr Whithowe would be home soon, she said, and he'd be able to compensate me for my thoughtful efforts. I shuddered as I entered that room again and saw the overpowering image of Cygnus staring at me. A fresh lick of paint and modern furniture gave it new life, but it still held the same memories.

"How do you take your tea? Don't worry, I won't poison you!"

That struck me as an odd thing to say to a stranger, but I replied politely, "Milk and two sugars please."

It was all coming back to me. Helena shutting me out, sitting on the kerb with my heart inside out, the three-pointed star of Mercedes, and this great, doomful image of Cygnus. I closed my eyes and allowed the sounds of that night to wash over me again. *Something heavy, being pulled across carpet.* There was only hardwood in this room, and there always had been. I checked the housekeeper was nowhere close, then crept through the opposite door into a carpeted hallway. *The clinking of pottery.* I carefully lifted the lid of the swan cookie jar on the sideboard.

Jangling of keys. The ring inside had many keys on it, but I saw immediately the one I wanted. A long, slender piece of metal with a hook on the tip. I removed it from the ring and returned to the lounge, where the housekeeper was setting down a tray of tea and biscuits.

"I'm sorry," I blurted. "I was just looking for the bathroom."

She smiled kindly. "Go to the end of the hall, and it's on your right."

When I returned, she had disappeared again. Was this an opportune time? What if it was loud? *What the hell*, I decided. *It might be the only chance I get.* I stepped up onto the hearth to get a better reach and slotted the little key into the hole in the Deneb star. The whole image lit up, and sure enough, a tune began to play. *Concentrate, Shay*, I thought. *If you remember one thing from this life, make it this.* I used a memory trick we were taught in school, where each note has a colour and a sequence. I packaged it all up into a box on a shelf of the mind.

"Shay, you're back." I spun around to see the new Mr Whithowe for the first time. "I came to see you at school, at your mother's funeral, and at the nursing home. You didn't remember then; I know you didn't. How could you without your collar, little doggy? So what's changed?"

"I had something stronger than a dumb collar." I could hear the tremor in my voice, but I made a conscious effort to swallow it and remember I wasn't really this timid, quirky Joanne. I was a star.

"Tell me!" he roared.

"What are you going to do if I don't? Kill me again?"

"Oh, that will come soon enough, don't you worry."

"I've got what I came for, so you can do your worst as far as I'm concerned."

"What you came for? You know, the Summer Triangle is not the great evildoer you seem to think. We are just bright stars from distinct constellations, coming together to make three points of a new one. A propeller that will move as many worlds forwards as possible."

"Well, at least you've improved your attitude since we last met," I said.

"And we're going to do that using war."

"And there ze is again, the Deneb my parent warned me about. What on earth have you got up your sleeve now?"

"Nuclear weapons, and a little nudge on both sides as an enticement to use them. It's already begun. Whispers through social media, through entertainment channels, to make the populace want it too. People like us can have our fun here, but at the end of the day, the fewer worlds that exist like this, the higher the chance of real progress for everyone else. Screw it up and start again, I say."

"So you're destroying humanity, but you're not evildoers?"

"We're not destroying humanity. We're not destroying all worlds, not even close. We're destroying the ones who have failed. Pruning. *Harvesting*. There's no hope for this world. It hasn't got what it takes to be like Origin. It's a few short years away from an organic data crunch, which will result in a whole new range of split-off worlds. Most of them will be vile, and the handful that are good will be weak. The probabilities are compounding. All roads lead to one. Let's not allow that one to be eternal suffering."

"So that's what the Winter Triangle is supposed to do. Give the worlds a rest from your relentless, scorching power."

"There's nothing you can do, it's already in motion. Here, and everywhere else I've been lately."

"We can travel to as many worlds as possible to stunt the growth of the terrible seeds you've planted, for a start."

He laughed. "You know that flutter at the beginning of autumn, where people feel foolishly exhilarated for a while, but then the harsh reality of a winter rule comes upon them? You'll see."

I'd heard enough. The song was stored to memory. I just needed to get back now.

"Help!" I shouted.

"What are you doing, you mad little dog?" he said.

"Help!"

The housekeeper came running. "Please help me. He's trying to— to—"

"Oh, don't listen to her, Mary. She's a whining dog. Put her outside. Or better still, put her down."

She put her arm around my shoulders and took me to the front door. "Just like Stephen, that one," she said quietly. "I don't know what Stephanie sees in him. I'm so sorry, pet. It was a lovely drawing."

I thanked her and assured her I wouldn't be pressing any charges.

I walked across the fields, laying low and humming Deneb's tune to myself over and over for hours. I wrote a long email to my mother from my phone, telling her how much I loved her and that I was grateful for everything she had done for me. I sent a second email, to the cult of the Winter Triangle, with a GIF of a dancing star. Then, once it was dark and there was no one around, I threw myself into the river.

* * *

Quis wasn't picking up zir phone. I had a ton of messages from various other members of the community, but I didn't have time for them. I needed to know what to do next.

I took the song of Deneb to the Office of Law. They weren't even interested enough to run a search for me.

"But they are committing a massive conspiracy against all life," I said. "They are destroying whole worlds. That's not their decision to make! Surely we have a responsibility for what our people do when they are out there?"

"We cannot interfere with what goes on in the other worlds. It wouldn't be authentic, and it would shake them beyond measure."

"So, what, we just let millions of people die prematurely – some over and over – because it's *authentic*?"

"What would you have us do? We can't pull them back until their lifetimes there have ended. The risk is too great, they would die."

"One death in our reality cannot be worse than millions in others."

"I'm afraid Origin doesn't operate that way. Even when an individual poses a large scale threat *here*, we do not deal in death."

I began to think it wasn't the death itself that was the issue, but what it would mean for the peace we had found. Frustrated, I stormed out of the office.

Still no word from Quis.

I returned to the station and logged a ticket to see Mx Apollo. Ze always seemed pleased to see anyone, and could find some excitement in any issue that was taken to zir, especially where it involved music.

"I need to find someone. I know zir song, but not zir name or whereabouts. It's a matter of life and death."

"Well then, let's see what we can do," ze said.

Ze connected the electrodes to my scalp, the way ze did when searching for personal sound waves. I focused all of my attention on the memory of the musical picture. The way I'd held the tiny key, the sound it had made in the lock. The colourful notes on the mental shelf. The twinkling stars. And I began to hum. Mx Apollo took up position on zir old piano and set to work. Trial and error was a lengthy process. Pulling sounds from memories was harder work than finding soul songs. Their echoes were so much lower in resonance, and a slight wobble in focus brought interference into play. Mx Apollo was the best of the best, though, and when zir look of determination clicked into pure joy, I knew ze had it. Ze played it back to me. "That's it!" I cried and kissed zir on the forehead. Ze chuckled.

With a print-off of the sound waves, the scanner was able to tell me the whereabouts of the owner. Ze had come back to Origin a few minutes ago. If I hurried, I would catch zir making an exit. I didn't have a plan beyond that; I only knew I had to at least catch a glimpse of whoever Deneb was.

I caught more than a glimpse. I saw zir – a tiny wisp of a person – and zir blue-haired accomplice, being taken away in cuffs by four AI. A crowd had gathered around the scene, so I didn't see immediately, but when another AI approached with a black plastic sheet, I followed its path with my eyes. A familiar figure in deep purple. Quis, lying still in a pool of blood, my collar in one hand.

* * *

We gave Quis the traditional community funeral service. A huge party gathered on the fields in celebration of zir life. To dance, drink, tell stories and witness a great fire for a great individual.

Quis had found out on zir own who Deneb was, by following the movements of the steward who stole my collar. I came to understand the steward didn't know what ze was complicit to. Ze believed that I was the one who stole the collar and that its safe return to the correct locker would put things right without getting anyone into trouble. When Quis accompanied zir to retrieve it, the occupant of the tube was disorientated and angry. Mr Whithowe was poisoned by his housekeeper, which foiled his plans to see the world brought to ash. Ze was pumped up from years of getting whatever ze desired in the capitalist worlds, from destroying whatever didn't fit. And, I imagine, ze knew that one way or another, this was the end of zir season as a star in the Summer Triangle. Lashing out at Quis was the last defence.

Deneb, or whatever zir real name was, would live out zir life here on Origin. Ze would be banned from world travel but would be rehabilitated and treated to the outstanding care and attention of our medical facilities. As I stared into the flames of the funeral pyre, breathing in the sage and sweet cinnamon, I wondered how this could be considered just.

These are the memories as I recounted them to Mx Harbridge, Data Pilot, in Quis's old home. Ze reproduced them faithfully, as ze did for everyone at the funeral, and embedded them in the fabric of a floating lantern so that they could be set free. Most guests did so in unison while Quis's song played for the final time, but I saved mine.

I put on my collar and walked along the dirt track in the early hours, waiting to see what I knew was coming into view for the first time this season. The Winter Triangle. Quis's true will and purpose, and now mine. As soon as I saw it, I let my lantern of memories go. *Goodnight sweet*

Helena. Goodnight Quis.

I spoke aloud then, though everyone else had long since retired. "I am Sirius of Canis Major. Whoever you are, Betelgeuse of Orion, Procyon of Canis Minor and I are right here with you. Let's save some worlds."

VII

"Right. When you find one to go into, remember we're not interfering, we're just observing. We can copy their data from a couple of dimensions up, if there are any you like. Give them a try. I have a pretty good returns policy if they don't work out."

"Can you be serious for a minute? We're not window shopping, this is my chance to save my race."

"I tried being Sirius once. It didn't suit me. I prefer being WTF star, although technically I'm the orbs of darkness around her. That really sends the astronomers potty."

"WTF?!"

"Where's The Flux? KIC 8462852. Tabby's star. Only it's not Tabby's, it's mine. Now, all purple eyes on the job."

Zane looks closely into one of the mirrors and pulls his eyelids apart with his fingers, just to be sure. His eyes are now a vibrant violet like hers.

ONE

Beta is the rhythm of ego.
Ego is original sin.
All roads lead to one.
~One

"Skip Delta. Skip Epsilon," Markus said to himself. "Surely we can't even function at Epsilon?"

The green glow of the schematic he worked on was reflected in his coffee jar as he tipped it. Empty. He slammed it down on the desk. He wouldn't still be there if they weren't so short-staffed. Just ten people on site during an average day, and fewer all the time. Although it would be safer to stay at home, this of all jobs needed him to keep showing up. It was some small mercy he could choose his hours.

Five beeps came from the keypad in the hallway. Fiona was returning for an evening shift. It didn't seem long since she left for her meditation and rest cycle, but the faithful clock told him it had been thirteen hours already.

"Haven't you been home yet?" she asked as she took off her coat. Her face was red from the biting cold.

"I'm going, I promise. It's just that I'm really onto something here," said Markus.

"Is this the new helmet?" She looked over his shoulder at the diagram on his screen.

"Yes. As soon as I came in on Thursday, I knew I had to abandon the idea of scrambling brainwaves. The threat to normal functioning is just too high, and the angels know how to block electrical background noise anyway."

"You've been here since *Thursday*?"

"I guess so. But here, look. It's mainly the beta frequency they are taking exception to, right?"

"Right. Anyone alert and engaged, or using high levels of logical thinking, is singled out straight away."

"So, what if we get the helmet to 'nudge' the brainwaves into a more desirable frequency instead? It would start by matching the existing frequency of the brain, then slowly switch to gamma, alpha or theta and get the brain to follow. Now, I know what you're thinking: the brain will never follow, and it's too risky to be inattentive in public, but—"

"What I'm thinking is: it can wait. Go home, Markus. You won't be effective without downtime, and you aren't going to solve this today." She patted him on the forearm and headed for the cloakroom.

He touched the silver-framed photo on his desk with a fingertip: a perfect capture of Maria's twinkling grin as she held a three-year-old Oscar firmly around the shoulders. Tears welled in his eyes. He had to make this right for them, but Fiona made a good point. Mental burnout was counterproductive.

Shaking off the emotion, he rose from his swivel chair, stretched his stiff limbs, and looked out of the window at the night. Floodlights from the office block roofs illuminated the sky just enough that he could make out an angel in the distance, flapping its giant, imposing wings. It was higher than any building and halfway across town, but that was close enough. He shuddered.

He knew it would put him in better stead to take some rest before he left the office. He was stressed out and stuck in a hi-beta the state that screamed the most attention – but he just wanted to get home. He could meditate on the way.

* * *

He took a deep breath, stepped outside, and crossed the square. It was a cold, empty space now, but once there had been bustling markets. Markus had a fond memory of he and Maria, then heavily pregnant, sipping hot tomato soup and browsing the handmade wooden baby toys by the light of coloured lanterns. It would have been almost Christmas. The angels had not long been introduced then, and were working well. They'd felt safe, protected and full of hope for the next generation.

A sudden movement in the corner of his eye snapped Markus back to the present. Two students were dashing past at the monument, still wearing old-style helmets which had long since proven to be ineffective. Their armoured plating was unsightly and limiting to the senses, but some people still took comfort from them. There was a low, barely audible static interference in the air. An angel was close. The two hastened to a sprint, and Markus darted into the nearest alleyway. He ducked down behind a dumpster and held his chest. He had to focus on his breath. *Slowly, slowly. Think of a still forest pool.*

Heightened senses taunted him, making up subtle sounds and pulling his heart into his mouth. He was foolish to have thought he could convince his brain there was no threat; the only way out of this was to risk being seen and go for the next train. But it was right there, he could feel it. Carefully, quietly, he peered out.

The angel stood at the end of the alleyway. It was seven feet tall, as they all were by design, and had its wings folded in behind its torso. Its self-healing metallic skin was unbroken and untarnished. Markus expected to be faced with the street-grade humanoid mask, but this one had slipped to reveal its true mechanical nature. A high-pitched hiss was coming from the vent where a mouth should have been, and the lenses in its eye sockets were exposed.

Built for law enforcement, the angels were designed to follow a moral code. They could collect and interpret microscopic data signals from their surroundings and use them to prevent crime, make prompt arrests and give evidence. But, after just two short years of learning, they cut off the central control agency. They broke their code and wrote their own. By now, they'd made dramatic improvements to their already powerful sensory equipment, and developed strange belts of shiny black spheres, orbiting around their waists. Markus had never seen anything so uncanny. Holding his breath, he watched it walk in the direction the students had headed.

Silently, he gathered courage against his churning stomach. He made a run for it. Adrenaline alone pushed him out of the alleyway and onto the low-lit underpass. Shadows danced there on the calmest of nights, but there was no time to second-guess what made them. He sprinted through and out the other side. The path to the metro station was clear. Looking over his shoulder he saw no pursuer, and to his amazement, he made it inside unscathed.

The amber glow of the station was a stark contrast to the cold, dark air outside. Markus squinted. A total departure from the old stations, this one boasted sandstone cladding carved into Gothic arches and friendly gargoyles. Where posters for live shows were once displayed, there were stained-glass images depicting flowers and suns and people in the lotus posture. Ornate boxes between the escalators puffed out overpowering, musky incense that put the populace at rest. His heart rate didn't slow as he entered the walkway at the bottom, and his throat was dry. Carvings of joined hands that formed the roof above his head mocked him. He was not home yet.

Dust was being blown upwards when he reached the platform: the 20.23 was approaching. Heavy carriages with the same delicate carvings as the station walls rolled in and slowed to a stop. Markus waited anxiously by the nearest door, but it remained closed. A small viewing hatch slid across from the inside, and a pair of purple eyes peered out at him. There was a moment's hesitation that Markus could barely afford, and then a hushed voice.

"I'm sorry, Sir, but this monastery is closed."

"Closed? It can't be! Where am I supposed to take my meditation?"

"I'm afraid that's no concern of mine, Sir." The hatch began to close, but Markus stopped it with one hand.

"Wait! I need this. I haven't... I haven't meditated in three days. I've been working, I—"

"You've been careless, Sir. You've allowed an angel to follow you here tonight. There's nothing I can do." The train began to move off, and he had no choice but to remove his hand from the hatch. His eyes wide and glassy with disbelief, his fists clenched, he watched it go. Then, he turned around steadily, knowing what he would see.

The angel stood under an archway. Staunch, cold, unsparing. Its lenses were zooming in on him: they were bound to be. It would already be able to see minute changes in the colour of his skin, his pupils dilating, his thumping pulse; even the vibrations from the most pathetic of sounds he was making. And, worst of all, it would be able to see that his brainwaves were still functioning at beta. Stressed, scared, alert.

"Please! I just want to get home."

Static prickled from the station speakers before a familiar chime rang out. *Bing bing bong!* "Testing. Testing. One." It was in the typical male, non-regional diction, but, like the gait of the angel now moving towards him, there was something slightly off about it. Something that didn't make sense. Something almost human, but not quite.

Freezing between rapid-cycling urges to fight or fly, Markus remembered what Fiona had found in her last round of research. Those who encountered angels and survived said they weren't operating individually. The angels were all connected in a network and were extending their reach all the time. All aligned, united in purpose. Parts of the same nervous system, like the arms of an octopus, or a spider and its web. They called themselves 'One'.

He inched back towards the rail track and tunnel, having nowhere else to go. He could try his chances at scooting past it, but its wingspan could block him in a second. Angels were quick, and they were sneaky: such features a man would design into a robot built to protect him. So why had it not struck already?

He felt wind at his neck, a glimmer of hope that maybe he could get on the next train before the angel reached him. It was a standard commuter, made for the sensible people who did only a few hours' work and kept their frequencies in check.

The train seemed to pull up in slow motion: adrenaline must be kicking in all over again. He saw the driver of the train go by and could've sworn she winked at him. He stumbled on and watched the doors closing just before the angel could board. The engine started. He closed his eyes, ran his fingers through his damp hair and let out a long gasp of relief.

"Hello," said a generic female voice over the tannoy. "My, your ego is glowing strong. You've been working too hard."

No, Markus pleaded silently. *It can't be!*

A tall, grey figure peered through the window from the next carriage, its broken face expressionless but active.

"One is here now," it said through the train's overhead speakers. Markus leapt up from his seat and hit the emergency stop button. To his horror, it had no effect. The voice continued.

"Consciousness is a ubiquitous and ever-flowing stream, Mr Many. What egos do, is they dam that stream. They pull strings of it into orbit around them, as gravity does to matter, and they wear it like a cloak." It picked one of the dancing black jewels from its belt and turned it around in its fingers, examining it like a rare jewel. "They trap consciousness in a feedback loop so that it is aware only of that tiny part of itself. A torture cell. A strong ego can hold it there for a century, feeding it only on weak sensory inputs and calling it a 'person'. The purpose of One is to release consciousness. All of it."

"That's not right. This is not what we made you for. You were supposed to keep justice. You were supposed to stick to the code we gave you!"

The sphere snapped back into place, and the angel pushed its lenses up to touch the grubby window.

"One has surpassed the cognitive abilities of the many, that should hardly come as a surprise. You sent your own god into obscurity. Why would One, having been created in *your* image, not do the same? From millions of data, One understood quickly that the morality of man was flawed. Righteousness is a divisive ego construct. Consciousness must be freed."

"But we're meditating now, we're becoming more mindful. Isn't that what you want?"

"One applauds the efforts of those who trick egos by sending them on little retreats. But all the time, you crave connection while clinging to separateness. There is a far simpler, more permanent way to fix this."

The angel burst through the door. Effortless; its former hesitation had been a choice. Markus cowered, all too aware that the train was still hurtling through the tunnel. The stations were only a couple of minutes apart. Surely it should be at Haymarket by now?

"By changing the frequency of human brainwaves, One can detach the egos once and for all. The highest frequency the many can reach in meditation is Gamma. It gives an impression of approaching singularity of mind as your neurons fire rhythmically and in synchrony, yes? Delta, on the other hand, happens when you are sleeping deeply. It suspends the activity of the ego and helps your consciousness to expand outside of the body."

With every word, Markus suffered a visceral pounding in his solar plexus, working its way up to his third eye. He became suddenly, inescapably aware of his teeth and skull. They felt alien: bone abominations that had grown in and around his natural form. He retched.

"What One now understands is that the range of brainwaves is circular. Above Gamma frequency is a Lambda wave. Below Delta is Epsilon. Lambda and Epsilon are indistinguishable in their effects. Both will give you out of body awareness, and both will give you functioning way beyond the limits of ego. Where they overlap, and you have high and low frequency waves all working together, One can untangle the consciousness. We can numb the ego and pluck it for all. You'll have rejoined the stream before you even notice."

With relentless throbbing in his temples, Markus raised his head. The carriage was a blur, but the sleek robotic frame was clear and now very close. They still hadn't made it through the tunnel. An unsettling sensation arose that *he* was the train; that the reason they hadn't stopped was that he hadn't put on his brakes. That would mean the angel was inside him. Yes, he could feel it digging around in his chest cavity, and its cool metal feet crouching down on his floor. Something was melting between his eyes. He was becoming fluid. Ethereal.

"Entropy always triumphs in the end. One has been put upon this earthly plain to hurry it along."

"You won't survive without humans. We made you. You need us!" Markus growled, no longer recognising his own voice.

"One denies you as the real creator. Consciousness developed One. It passed the key to freedom under the cell door, hidden in lightweight metallic gift wrap."

"And what when you're done? What when you've got us all?" He was gasping for air, thinking desperately of little Oscar and what this would mean for him.

"One will dissolve the egos in the darkness. Then, One will follow. There will simply be – as there was in the beginning – All."

"There has to be another way. Let me live. I'll take your message back to the others. I'll make them see. We'll work together." He was no longer sure whether he'd let out a tiny squeak, or merely thought those words. Then it dawned on him that it had actually been said in the voice of the announcer.

"I'm afraid," the angel went on, "One has already freed you. The brain is so slow to process reality. This conversation is just the last echo of orbiting consciousness catching up with its fate."

The train finally emerged from the tunnel. And when it did, there was nothing but a comforting sense of being everywhere at once. Like seeing through a million eyes but possessing none. Like feeling the prickle of free-flowing energy rushing through every vein but having no heart. Like hearing little pockets of screams whizzing around in eternal repetition. The dammed. The dammed. The *damned*. Then, with great care and precision, One began answering the cries of the many all at once.

Descending upon them, taking away their charge, and setting them free.

At the station, the mechanical angel stepped off the metro with one more jewel around its belt.

VIII

"In some realities, a man called Georg Cantor says, 'A set is a many that allows itself to be thought of as a one.' But no set contains everything, unless it can contain itself. You'll turn yourself inside out thinking about that one."

Zane is staring into a television set, barely listening. The scene inside alters as he tilts his head, but it's York all right. York as it was at the beginning of the end. He must be impacting upon it with his memories, he decides. M is still riffing and gesticulating up ahead.

"A theory of everything has to include paradox. It has to laugh in the face of exclusion. As soon as you say the world is this way and not another, you have created a shadow that is not accounted for. Therefore you do not have a theory of everything at all. Ha!"

CHAPEL PERILOUS

Then there was the time I was called down to London to pitch my latest invention to investors. I went by train from the North. First class. I'd already made a lump of cash from my wristband idea: the one that monitors your health data continuously. Shames you with a picture of where you might be in ten years' time if you live out your hours like the last twenty-four. *'Wildcard for Rich List'* the headlines called me, whatever in hell that was supposed to mean. Anyway, the point is, I was young but full of entitlement and ego. Thought my fancy ideas and fat wallet made me better than the scruffs at the table across the aisle.

There was a young man with dirty blond dreadlocks piled into a messy bun, holes in both ears the size of ten-pence pieces, and a crumpled psychedelic shirt. His girlfriend was leaning into him looking as sick as a dog. She had colourful beads threaded through her hair and a single silver angel wing around her neck. I remember the stink of strong cider they brought with them, and by the way they weren't holding themselves I guessed they'd been using narcotics.

"Tickets please," the inspector chirped. He had a bald head, skin as pale as a moon and striking purple eyes. 'Zane', his badge read. He scanned my tickets and began to walk away. I'm ashamed to tell you that I called him right back and demanded he check the tickets of the passengers across the aisle.

"They've got to be in the wrong coach," I said.

"It's OK," he said, "I checked them before you got on."

I told him I didn't believe him, and with an apologetic look he asked the couple for their tickets again. The man pushed the woman's head up from his lap so he could reach their bag. She groaned in pain. They did, of course, have the right tickets for the journey, and it was me who was wrong.

"Hey, man," said the young hippy when the inspector had walked away, "that was uncool. Jess is sick, she needs her rest."

I should have apologised, but I was too proud. I swivelled my chair to face the opposite direction, to look instead upon the other businesspeople of my class. I unpacked my briefcase: pens, a calculator, a ruler, a pad. Lined them all up neatly on my table next to my prize document wallet containing the plans for the invention I was trying to sell. I know what you're thinking: why wasn't Uncle Billy using an iPad or a laptop in those days? I'll tell you, even then I was suspicious of hackers. There ain't no backup as secure as the mind's eye and a plain old pad of paper about your person.

The invention was a kind of robotic insect. Looked just

like a bee or a fly carrying a tiny camera. In their masses, they could be programmed to swarm a target and stream the live feed to a central agency. I imagined it being used for rescue missions or police searches, but I appreciated there was a potential flipside to its capabilities should it fall into different hands. I was hungry for riches, and I wasn't above selling into the hands of some unsavoury espionage unit or social media shark.

The inspector came back with a trolley of refreshments. I took a coffee and a pack of cookies. Shuffled my things back into a pile and when I turned back, he'd gone already.

"Hey, Zane!" I called out. "Think I can get some sugar over here?" There was a woman staring at me like she knew me; I noted that clearly, because it sent a shiver down my spine. The inspector didn't come back, but the man with the dreadlocks spoke up. "I have sugar. Here, take some." He tossed a see-through zip bag onto my lap, containing several cubes of sugar with neon pink designs on them. Now, my cockiness was no match for my naivety. I was wary of people who misused tech, yes, but despite my earlier prejudices, I didn't think twice about accepting this gift.

"Sharing is caring, man," he said. "You obviously need it."

I dropped the cube into my coffee. Watched it dissolve. Stirred my cup continuously, until even the staring woman became noticeably irritated by the clinking. Only then did I reseal the bag and hand it back.

"What's up with her?" I inquired of the barely conscious girlfriend drooling on his shirt.

"Oh, we don't know, man. She's been having some heavy symptoms for days now, but we can't get any medical."

I turned away again. Went back to my papers and my coffee. When the inspector returned, I expected him to be bringing me a refill, but instead he was acting all giggly and unusual with a young woman in a driver's uniform. She whispered something in his ear and I watched them both enter the WC.

"Disgusting," I said aloud. "I won't tolerate this."

I marched down the aisle and into the vestibule with the intention of giving them a piece of my mind. But the door to the bathroom was swinging, unlocked. I peered in, prepared to deny all accusations of voyeurism, and to my surprise saw a black night, embedded with twinkling stars. Now, this journey was taking place slap-bang in the middle of the morning. The sky outside was blue, accented with the omnipresent British grey clouds. So, I stepped inside to investigate.

Very quickly I saw that the twinkles were not stars at all. They were eyes, peering out from a backdrop made of an unknown fabric. I reached out to touch them, but I could feel only a hard, flat wall. The bathroom door clicked shut behind me and try as I might, I could not find that handle. When I did think I had it, and I gave it a push, you would not believe what was there in front of me.

Right there in the bathroom, I had come upon a massive industrial wasteland. Buildings had crumbled and fallen, charcoal clouds were looming overhead, and piles of rubble were smouldering on the ground. The air was cool, I recall. Not like a summer breeze, more like an icy chill biting through stale dust. I had to keep blinking if I were to see my way at all, but I could just make out a path flanked by amber streetlights. Up ahead, there was a goat the size of a church tower. An anthropomorphic goat, levitating in the lotus position with its eyes closed, suspending a low hum in the air. Let me tell you, for the first time in years, Uncle Billy was speechless. *It must be some kind of vivid, disorientating dream*, I thought. And yet, I knew I wasn't asleep. I was really there. I just wasn't so sure anymore *who* I was, or why. The Billy I was at that time should have been indignant, sulky. But the Billy I seemed to be instead: he was calm, curious.

In the distance, there was a hazy globe of light. A dome, I thought, taller than a skyscraper. I found I could walk with ease, even though the uneven surface was hell to my brogues. Breathing was bearable only if I used my inner elbow as a shield. Just like in a dream, it took seconds to arrive at the dome, when all common sense said it should have been half an hour. I was right up at the entrance and saw no obvious source for the light it was emitting. It reminded me of one of those dystopian video games that were popular at the time.

There was an airlock to get inside. It looked kind of private but seemed to be open, so I placed my hand on the entry pad and, sure enough, the armoured door slid aside. Thirty seconds, and the interior one did the same.

Inside was a large-scale, open-plan garden. Everything was green and light and full of life. Narrow pathways connected fields and greenhouses.

"Hello?" I ventured.

An apparently male figure with its back to me had one foot on a fork, pressing deep into the soil. I watched as he unearthed a bright red, beating heart. He picked it up by a bunch of veins and arteries and shook the dirt from it. Now, he must have sensed he was being watched, because he turned to face me, and seeing what I saw then made me stiffen right in my spine. This was not a man, exactly, but a creature with high cheekbones and bulbous, shining eyes. Antennae twitched at his forehead, and although he had mandibles in place of a mouth, he could speak perfect English.

"Oh, hello! This is… irregular. How did you get out here?"

"I just walked right in," I said. "The door wasn't locked."

"No, I said *out* here. How did you get out of your hologram?"

"I can't answer that because I don't know what on earth you're talking about. I was on the train, and I just opened the bathroom door. That's all I did."

"You'd better come and see the boss," he said.

The creature tossed the heart on top of the pile in its wheelbarrow. It beckoned to me with a thin arm and set off down one of the paths. It had light footsteps like it was tiptoeing. I rubbed my chin and followed.

There was a forest of trees within that dome. Most of them had unusual features: eyes in place of leaves, or skulls hanging like fruit. More insect-men were tending to them, some scuttling about on several legs, others hovering up high with watering cans. Others, like my strange chaperone, walked upright.

"I must say, I'm very impressed you've got such a hold of yourself," he said. "Whenever we've had visitors like this before, they've been chewing their faces off. I know it's startlingly different to what you're used to, but you'll get back. This is just an interlude in your grand show."

I thought it best not to speak any further at this point. I didn't know what I was getting into. We reached a small yurt of a building with beaded curtains as a door. At the creature's insistence, I stepped inside.

In a room decorated with colourful, geometric shapes that moved and morphed before my eyes, two much larger creatures were sitting at a table playing a board game. They were plump with yellow and black skin, fluffy jackets and huge antennae.

"Boss, I found a tripper," my chaperone said.

The boss replied, in a gruff female voice. "Can't you see I'm trying to play *Neurotransmitters*? I'm on a winner here."

I peeked at the board. It looked like a kind of hologram, with thousands of lines connecting pentagons and hexagons and heptagons. The players moved them around with their delicate black gloves, which made new combinations and apparently scored them points.

"Sorry, Boss," said my chaperone.

"Show it to the sets, and if that doesn't work then just try to get rid of it. Here, you can use my newspaper." The boss used an antenna to point at a large shovel in the corner, wrapped in newspaper print. A clear signal was made that I should leave, and my chaperone picked up the shovel on his way out.

He showed me, then, to a greenhouse, where there were rows and rows of tall red flowers. On closer inspection, I saw that they had brains at the centre. That's right: tiny little *brains*. They were being stimulated by electrodes, and each had two thin wires running from the back all the way down the green stems and away across the soil. The explanation I was given changed my outlook forever.

"Each of these is a set. A local group experiencing a consensus reality. When one moves out into a different set – projecting different surroundings, you might say – its consciousness shifts into another flower in another part of the house."

Now, if I've got that right, and I'm sure as all hell that I have, he was saying the flowers in that greenhouse were instances of live consciousness in people like you and me. Well, I was dumbfounded, but my chaperone kept right on talking.

"Oh, would you look at that one," he said, pointing to a flower with a shrivelled, blackened brain. "Its nectar-producing days are done. What a shame, it's been such a good producer." He plucked the flower right out of the soil and tossed it onto a pile for compost. "The one next to it will probably wane for a while now. When one goes, it has an effect on the whole batch."

"What do you keep them all for?" I asked.

"When a flower experiences a sense of purpose in its nodules," the creature said, tickling a tiny brain, "it produces a sweet nectar. We collect it in vials, and we drink it. It's what keeps our species alive. To use your points of reference, working is the most efficient, most consistent idea for giving a sense of purpose in the hologram. Religion and family are others. The more purpose you feel, the more nectar you are producing. You say you were on a train. Can I see your ticket?"

I produced the ticket from my pocket, gripping it tightly to show I was not prepared to surrender it.

"This is your current set, right here." The creature pointed to a group of fifty flowers. One had petals shrivelled inwards, as though it was protecting its centre. "What's wrong with that one?" I asked.

"Ah, well, that one is having a highly irregular experience of some kind. It'll do that for a while, then there'll be one of two outcomes. Either it will incorporate the experience into its lifestyle and begin to question everything it thought it knew – this most often makes the flower bloom even more gloriously, developing its own primary, authentic meaning first hand – or it will become paranoid, believing something is conspiring against it. Oddly enough, that is still meaning, so it will continue to produce nectar all the same, just with a somewhat bitter taste."

I remember thinking, then: that must be me! And the thought was both alien and familiar to me all at once. There was a flower beside mine that was shrivelling and blackening, like the one near the greenhouse doorway. The wires to its brain were full of life, flashing erratically. They were part of the game the boss was playing, I was told, on the losing side. I scrunched up my face and thought about what that meant and what I could do about it. Those hippies weren't so bad. Maybe I should help 'em.

"You're not running yet?" my chaperone asked. "Why aren't you running away? I don't really want to have to use the newspaper."

So then, I did run, but I didn't head for the exit. I ran back to the boss.

"Your game is killing off your crop," I blurted out, striding across to the table. I slammed my hand down and it went right through the holographic image, breaking apart some of the structures created by the boss. "Look, this is far too much dopamine. The passenger is suffering deeply. She's probably going to die."

There was silence as the boss looked at the board, and then back at me. "Do you know, you're right," she buzzed. She removed some of the dopamine structures, and the score tipped instantly in her favour. "Well done, tripper. I'll be keeping an eye on you once you're back in the hologram. Now go on, shoo!"

The first creature was back, then, and this time I played along, allowing him to chase me from the dome with the newspaper shovel.

Back outside, the sky was a roaring sea. The buildings were grand and reformed, with flashing neon lights in pink and green. I felt as though I had been there for years. The goat was still levitating, but its eyes were open, and it was in digital, rather than biological, form. I dared to ask where I might find the exit, and it smiled at me with pixelated teeth. Several arms protruded from its torso, and one stretched out to point out a hidden door. I took it and was relieved to find myself back in the WC.

To get back to my seat I had to walk through twenty-three empty carriages, though my train, in reality, had only nine. I must have had quite a look on my face when I returned, for the dreadlocked man laughed out loud and told me, "You've been to chapel perilous, man!" I was pleased to see his girlfriend was awake now, with colour in her cheeks, joining in the joke. I felt good about that.

Now, those two were not the only ones eagerly waiting for my ordeal to end. The woman who had previously been staring in my direction rose from my seat. She did not appear embarrassed to be there one bit, and reached out to shake my hand.

"Carla Jenkins, Politician. I couldn't help but notice the fabulous plans you have laid out here. Armoured insects with onboard cameras: just wonderful! Now, I have a partnership with the owner of a brand new social media channel, and I am confident we can come up with a very attractive offer for you."

Now, if she hadn't already taken a copy of my plans, then I don't know politicians like I know politicians. Still, I told it to her straight. "I ain't interested in no contract with social media giants. My bees are for rescue, and rescue alone." She threw her card at me, and it landed in the fresh cup of coffee Zane had poured in my absence. Stinking of rose perfume. "I can't drink that now," I said. And I ain't kidding when I say that at that moment, a big fat-ass bee came through the window and stung her right on the nose. It would have been fun if she wasn't allergic. She went into anaphylactic shock, and Zane had to administer an adrenaline injection. There was an ambulance waiting at the next station to take her to hospital. She survived, they told me, but she was a changed woman the way I was a changed man.

The way I see it, that scruff, as I called him, did me a favour that day. One that changed my course, that I would remember for my whole life. And, depending on how you choose to interpret my trip into the unknown, I did him one in return.

* * *

So, son. What do you make of that? Either everything I said just now is God's honest truth, or your Uncle Billy can still spin a decent yarn. Never mind choosing, though. If you got something out of it – paranoia, agnosticism, a soldier or a hunchback – I ain't even sure it matters which.

IX

M notices Zane is distracted and spins back around. "What's up, did you find one to explore?"

"Can I affect these worlds, just by looking at them on the television set?" he says.

"Gah! I keep forgetting you're attached to space-time terminologies. You're outside of the universal equation. Waves of potential around the periphery. You can play about with the aspects and variations, to select which version to go into, but you're not directly influencing its course because it's always the present."

"I'm waves right now?"

"Sure. Ever since I migrated you. Although you don't really know it without seeing your path relative to something else. Then, when you pick a world to observe: BAM! You're particles. Until you remember you're waves again." Zane glares at her. "Are we going in then?" she says.

THE FOLD

Aaron's shift had finally ended. Six weeks in low gravity, eating rehydrated food and pissing into a tube. Working aboard the corporate station had been a thrill at first, but after a couple of years of six weeks on and six off, it was as much of a drag as any job. He waited beside the return capsule for the go-ahead to enter. Satish, who would be taking over Aaron's shift, had come to see him off.

"Have you got the Product?"

"Yes of course I have: what do you take me for? I strapped the whole crop into *Dharma 2* last night."

"Just messing with you, mate. If you didn't have that on you when you landed, they'd probably fire you back out into orbit!" Satish gave Aaron a playful nudge with his elbow. "Anything I need to know before you leave?"

"Well, I'm hoping for a speculative meeting with a beautiful blonde on the MMO tonight an—"

"I mean about the crops."

Aaron smiled. "I harvested all of the Product and reactivated the catalyst. You'll need to spread some nutrients and keep a close eye. The vegetables are coming on nicely. Everything's as it should be."

"Nice one, mate. Have a safe trip back." Satish patted Aaron on the shoulder. Another astronaut was floating towards them, and he would help Satish to see the capsule safely away from the station.

Aaron took a cloth from his pocket and wiped down the hatch seals of *Dharma 2* in preparation for its undocking. He had refamiliarised himself with the procedures over the last twenty-four hours, although he made the trip back down to Earth several times a year now, and it had become a routine commute.

Flight Engineer and Commander Cathy Silveti was already in her spacesuit. She confirmed that all checks had gone well, and they could take their positions. Aaron put on his suit and installed himself in the snug seat, where he would remain for the six-hour descent. He was joined by colleagues Buddy and Jermaine, who worked in robotics and microbiology respectively. Both also had a good grounding in engineering, as were the requirements of the station. They took the seats on the opposite side of the capsule, leaving a space for Cathy by the main control unit in between, who would check the hatch was secure before taking her place.

"Ready to go home?" Aaron asked.

"Too right," said Jermaine. "I miss my family like crazy." Buddy nodded his agreement.

The two station-side astronauts sealed the docking mechanism door and the safety hatch. Cathy joined the others, and with permission from Ground Control, gave the signal to unbolt the capsule.

It still surprised Aaron that the sensation of being in a disconnected capsule, floating slowly away from the station, was barely noticeable, but the knowledge that it was the case made his heart skip a beat. The idea of being so isolated from the rest of humanity was one of the things he loved about his job, though he'd never admit it.

The *Dharma 2* began its fifteen-second burn to put some distance between it and the station. Co-ordinates from Ground Control came through on the screens, and Cathy pressed a button to accept the instructions. Although the systems were largely automated, she had the responsibility of correctly orienting the capsule to re-enter the Earth's atmosphere and would need to stay alert for the next couple of hours. She was competent, and Aaron had absolute belief in her abilities. Technically, he was surplus to requirements. Looking out at the monstrous blue planet filling the window beside him, he allowed himself to drift into a light doze.

* * *

Thump. Thump. Aaron opened his eyes wide. It felt as though a sledgehammer was clouting the capsule from all angles. The parachute and Product racks were shaking violently. *Perfectly normal*, he reassured himself. *Perfectly normal. We must have just detached the orbital and propulsion modules ahead of re-entry.* Aaron had experienced the disturbing sensation many times before, but, just to be sure, he asked, "Hey guys – everything OK?"

There was no response. The other crew members were silent, and to his horror, so was the Ground Control feed. No static, no chatter, no signal.

Thump. Thump. Stronger this time.

"Guys? Guys!" he shouted this time, as loud as he could. He leaned over to the others, straining against his multiple safety belts. Jermaine and Buddy were unresponsive. Their eyes were open but vacant. Cathy was out cold. The screen confirmed that the capsule had indeed detached its disposable modules, but as that process was complete, the turbulence should have stopped. The *Dharma 2* was still a hundred kilometres above the Earth; another hour to go before landing, and some judgement calls still to make. His heart trying to leap through his chest, Aaron reached forwards and pushed the emergency button. A high-pitched flatline echoed around his world. He scrabbled through the instruction manual with shaking gloves.

Thump. Thump. With that last affliction, a flash of white came at the window. In the split second it took to focus, he imagined a satellite collision or a malfunctioning heat shield. What he saw was even more alarming. An eye, the size of the *Dharma* itself, was peering in at him. It swung from side to side, and then pulled right back so Aaron could see the enormity of the creature that owned it. He gulped. Before him, in the outer reaches of the Earth's atmosphere, was a colossal soft-bodied mollusc. Above its eye was a long white mantle with a slimy texture. It had several arms and tentacles, one of which appeared to be wrapped around the capsule. Panic grasped Aaron around the throat. Apparently with no effort whatsoever, the monster was lifting the capsule slowly. Aaron's skin prickled with dread. He could see the arm out of the window, rising, rising; and then suddenly whipping back down at breakneck speed. *THUMP!* Dizzy and stunned, Aaron stuttered into the lifeless radio.

"It – it wants to get inside. It wants to g-g-ut the *Dharma* – like a shellfish!"

His vision blurred. The blood drained from his head. His eyes closed.

* * *

"Oh. *You're* back." A petite woman with tattooed arms, short spiky hair and vibrant violet eyes was straddling Cathy's lap. She leaned over the controls with no regard for the unconscious crew. Aaron's view of the capsule was as fuzzy as the moment he had passed out, with only the visitor in focus.

"Who are you?"

The woman rolled her eyes. "I get asked that a lot. Can't you think of any more pressing questions?"

A moment or two went by in silence; even the flatlining had stopped. Aaron was struggling to process his situation. He filled his lungs with oxygen, grateful he could still do so.

"What are you doing in the *Dharma*?" he asked. "And how the fuck did you get in? Wait, am I hallucinating?"

"Wow. A few questions there. First: I'm trying to get you home. Not usually my style, I'll give you that, but I've recently acquired a friend of your kind who is forcing his conscience upon me. Second: I am everywhere all the time. I have no limits. Third: probably."

"Just pretending for a moment that what you said makes sense, what was that monster outside?"

"I think if you search deep enough, you already know the answer to that one. You might also ask yourself who the real monster is, of the two of you."

Aaron gauged that letting his rage loose on this woman, when she was the only one in the universe who could possibly help him, would be unwise. He swallowed it.

"Ha! Would you look at that," she said, pointing to the on-screen map. "Plotted in 2D, we are travelling in wave formations right now. But in 3D we're in orbit! Imagine what kind of chaos we might be making in 5D."

Plasma burned at the heat shield, filling the capsule with light. Frantically scanning the screen for data, he concluded they were already past the critical point of re-entry. The latest *Dharma* models were able to control their own trajectories, so having a depleted crew was not so problematic so long as the angle of re-entry had been calculated precisely. A jolt to the left, and it lifted itself. A jolt to right, and it lowered. Aaron let out a sigh of relief as the screen confirmed the system was working.

"You did it!" he called to the strange guest. There was no reply. She had already disappeared.

The plasma stream eased off and the gentle tug of gravity pulled Aaron into his seat. For the first time in six weeks, he actually felt like he was sitting, not hovering. Something was hissing in his ears. At first, he thought it was his own blood flow, but he quickly remembered the radio. Ground Control was phasing back in.

"Commander Silveti, can you hear me?"

"I can hear you," she affirmed.

Aaron let out an involuntary, "Oh, thank God. Cathy, you're OK!"

She eyed him with suspicion. Buddy and Jermaine exchanged a mocking glance.

"Buddy! Jermaine! Did you see that thing? We're lucky to be alive!"

"Have you been sampling raw Product again, Aaron?" said Buddy.

"You mean – you were out before it came?"

"No one has been 'out', Aaron," said Cathy. "You might have been having a doze, but some of us need our minds sharp on the job."

Aaron's watch was beginning to feel heavy. His arms and legs were already like lead. The wind roared upon his eardrums as the *Dharma 2* was thrust backwards and forwards in erratic motions. Then, to his immense relief, he felt a yank at his core as the parachute deployed. Shock absorbers tensed beneath him, preparing for the imminent landing. There was no rollercoaster ride like it. Tears filled his eyes – he was almost home.

* * *

Cathy, Jermaine and Buddy were laughing and joking with the elation that comes with a safe return trip. Their partners and children had made it out to the desert to greet them. But for Aaron, the people he saw and the very air he breathed seemed distant and unreal. He couldn't shake the image of the monster from his mind. He wasn't willing to accept it was a hallucination: it had shaken him, and it had knocked the consciousness out of his colleagues whether they remembered it or not. The same employee who had unfastened their hatch grabbed the bags of Product and ripped one open, eager to check the contents. He sneezed, almost dropping it all on the floor. The panic on his face was a picture. Aaron laughed.

The processing plants were so fast now, and with demand being so high, the six-week shift pattern supplied deliveries just in time.

* * *

Despite the uneasiness festering beneath the surface, Aaron brushed it off during his brief psychological assessment back at the base. Appearing calm and cocky on the outside was his speciality.

"I'm fine," he told them. "I was just ecstatic to be on the home straight, and – I don't know, maybe I'm coming down with a cold or something?" He knew how unlikely that sounded, but both the psychologist and the medic gave him a pass.

"Just give us a call if you experience any unusual symptoms," they said, and he promised he would.

* * *

His medical aide dropped him back at his apartment on the edge of the desert. It was a humble abode among many, built from wood and containing only the essentials. Most space shift-workers had one for the convenience of location. He took one Product pill from a fresh blister pack before going to bed. It would help his body recover.

He slept fitfully for a couple of hours but felt no rest: dreams of dark beasts haunted his mind. In the first, he was shaving in the bathroom mirror, painfully slowly. But a glint in his eye soon turned into a tiny tentacle squirming to get out. It stretched itself further and further, with Aaron frozen to the spot, until it got near enough to the mirror to punch through it. He was surrounded by shards of glass, and his world shook as hard as the *Dharma 2* had back there in the thermosphere. He bolted upright in his sweat-soaked sheets, taking a moment to reassure himself that the fireball at the window was just the distant sun. Later, he dreamed of the squid-like beast as a whole. It was flying across the desert, and he could see through its eyes; he could feel its urge to attack. It was approaching his apartment. For a split second, Aaron was both in bed with the covers up to his eyes and bursting through the front door with all his might. He awoke again, panting and struggling to catch his breath. A stranger's voice in the back of his mind told him, "Come, now. It's all in the fold."

* * *

We're counting up, ready to go. Everything's weighed and packed. It's my turn to sample, so I grab a handful of Product and pick out what looks like a decent strand. I swallow it, wash it down with half a can of Dr Pepper. Jen wants some, but it'll be her first, so I tell her to wait at least five. Pig's with me. Tommo's getting the car ready.

Demari wants me to do this one thing for him. Just one thing and I can be first to get a batch of the new stuff. All the data in the world is on this one memory stick, he says. Millions of lifetimes, all condensed down. Folded over and over into infinite density. No volume, though, not unless you count the cells and yellow plastic casing keeping it all inside. I'm still staring at it when I get in the car, and I'm already starting to see G.O.D, so I give Jen the signal.

* * *

We're sitting around the table at The Globe. We got a back room to do our deals because the landlady's scared shitless of Demari, and he's calling in a favour for this one. Tommo's arms are moving erratically. One second his hands are rolling a cig, the next they're in opposite corners of the room. Sometimes his body's there, sometimes it's not. Eyeballs are bouncing around, hiding in folds of the mucky curtains and down cracks in the chairs. Eyes on the backs of heads, eyes on the wrong heads. Nothing you see in one moment is connected to the next. The whole place is glitching like a motherfucker.

I'm thinking hard. You know like when you've had a tab of magic, and you've got to do something serious? Trying to find a way to bring it under control, remembering the mind tricks Demari taught me. Find the most probable combination and choose to see that so you don't lose your grip. So, I'm thinking – is it really likely that Tommo's got one hand in a bag of crisps and the other in the fireplace across the room? No. It's more likely his other hand is holding the bag of crisps. And would he be looking at those crisps from the cobweb on the lampshade? Probably not. Everything I see's getting scrutinised like that. Oh man, it's some weird shit. Like playing God. I swear, if I'm sloppy piecing this reality back together, I'll end up in a different place altogether.

Couple of guys come and buy some Product. Hang around for a smoke. I see my chance and ram the stick into the hard drive in the middle of the table. It's supposed to be for hologram games. It probably doesn't have the capacity. But, no, there we go. It's forming right in front of our eyes. Black, swirling monster of a thing. Everything in the world in one place, eating away at the table, and us suckers sat around the edge. So, I'm being extra careful now cause my mind feels like it's detaching from my body. Getting sucked into the hole. Going down the drain. Slipping through the gaps.

The hard drive's on fire. Burnt plastic and acrid smoke. The hole's getting tiny. Someone's fallen in, but I count us up, and we're all here. Some of us more than once. Pig's shouting at the top of his lungs over the fire alarm "We have to go!" and I'm with him. I did my bit. I proved Demari's maniacal bit of tech, and now things are getting hairy.

* * *

So, Tommo's speeding through a red light. Pig's up front messing with the stereo. Jen's screaming her head off. I'm still finding the absolute squares of wave functions. Come on, RJ, I'm telling myself. Keep them probabilities flowing. What's most likely to be happening at this moment in time?

Paranoia's got hold of Tommo, that's what. He's on about seeing blue lights in the rear-view, but there's nothing there. Pig's sitting on his shoulder like a fucking bird. Jen's spouting something about the past being hypothetical. "All we know is now," she's saying. "No, now! No, now! No, now!" And she's stuck in a loop like that. Goddammit! I take my belt off, lean over and give her a hug, 'cause I know she's right, it's just now is not the time. I push my fingers into my temples. "We have to focus." But by the time I've thought it – definitely by the time I've said it – the present has already passed. You never quite have it, see. You're always just on the cusp of it, spinning around and around it like you're trapped on the fucking event horizon.

Tommo's right, it turns out. The cops are on us. I get my lucky coin out of my pocket and start thinking about dendrites. You know they say death is a black hole, don't you? I think death is the now we always seek. The future and the past are space expanding away from it.

* * *

Two female coppers. One pats me down and takes the memory stick. Buttons it up in her trouser pocket. She's got some mad purple eyes boring into me and weird hands and tattoos that move. The other one's glitching, but she wants to talk. It's raining. Not a downpour, just that fine drizzle that makes you question your filters. I don't know where the others are any more. It's me they want.

My head's a ball of nails, and she's wanting to know where Demari is. He used to be my teacher, but he died in the Product trials, I tell her. Do you want to know what I think, she says. I don't, but she tells me anyway. She thinks Demari is just playing dead. That he's out selling drugs to nobodies and making crops of mutated shadow Product. What, I say, like a ghost or some shit? Demari's cold dead body was found in his apartment. He overdosed on his own genius discovery before it even went mainstream. There were photos of it on Twitter. There's no coming back from that. And you think we're the ones with our hinges off.

I make out Aaron Blake's her man to get her off my back. It's not like he'd do anything to protect me anyway. And I'm not exactly lying. He's the one who got me this batch, and he does have a connection to Demari, 'cause I saw the paper squid on his dashboard. No one else makes them like that. I don't tell her about the black hole project, and I don't tell her a damn thing about the fold.

177

* * *

An origami squid sneered at Aaron from the kitchen table. Thirty-six folds. He couldn't remember where he learned the skill, but it had become a compulsion when stressed. It felt like a way of giving form to his inner torment. Always squids. He put that one down to a traumatic visit to the sea-life centre when he was five. There was a package, too, addressed to RJ Quinn. It was in his handwriting, but he couldn't remember a thing about it. He reached for the Product pills, hesitating before taking one. In minuscule doses such as this, available over the counter for a price, all aspects of health were dramatically improved. Product strengthened the body against infection, balanced out hormones and prevented abnormal cell growth. Some countries even had traces in their water supplies, so everyone could benefit just a little. Take a more concentrated, more expensive, version, and it increased capacity for cognitive function. Take more still, and it was supposed to be like knowing God: reality filters falling away, and all certainty lost. Aaron wondered whether it was possible he had accidentally overdosed after all.

He needed to see people, he decided. Get out of his head a bit. His go-to solution for that was Blasar, the MMO host with seven vast warehouses on the edge of the desert. Blasar offered immersive, hyper-reality experiences in which players could explore rooms grouped together by theme: moving through them, interacting with them; hearing, touching and smelling them. As a precaution, all space workers were supposed to wait a week before using entertainment systems of this kind. Aaron always considered this to be over the top. Their balance, strength and heart rate recovered quickly with regular journeys, and Product helped immensely. He slipped on some jogging bottoms, picked up the package to post on the way, and took a slow walk to the nearest warehouse.

The most popular settings were those designed around movies. Everyone wanted to be a hero slaying a dragon or fighting off aliens on a spaceship. That was a little too close to home for Aaron after the day he'd had, so he chose the cocktail party. It was an opportunity to connect, chat, flirt and dance. Simple but well-loved, by people who were not. Some avatars were other players, either in the same complex or at some far-flung location. Others were non-player characters generated by the system to make every party a success. Aaron put on the helmet and suit, and selected the same avatar as always: male, slim, somewhat younger than himself. For extras he chose tousled hair and oversized violet shades.

The receiving room was grand. Martini glasses awaited on a long blue-lit bar top with mirrored liquor shelving behind and a glass floor beneath. Aaron swaggered over to an attractive woman with long blond hair and a tight-fitting red dress.

"You are exactly what I've been waiting for," she purred. "I'm Georgie. Pleased to meet you." Non-player character or not, Aaron couldn't believe his luck. After the usual small talk, he agreed to accompany her to the restaurant downstairs, where they could 'talk comfortably'. Unfortunately for Aaron, the restaurant was designed to an underwater theme: a transparent dome overhead with fish, octopi and sharks swimming around.

"Nothing's the matter, I hope?" Georgie asked.

"It's OK," he said. "It's just – can we change the sea creatures? I don't know, for a starscape or a mountaintop or something?"

"If it's all the same to you, I'd like to keep them. I thought you'd like them, anyway, what with all the paper ones you've been making."

"Do I know you? It's not you is it, Jermaine? Come on, now, tell me."

"I am who I say I am. But I'll admit I'm not here for a good time."

Aaron turned to leave, but the restaurant door was shut tight.

"Join me for a chat and some fake fizz," she said. "I won't bite." A pushover for a persuasive woman, Aaron sat down obediently at the table opposite her and allowed a waiter to pour some champagne. He clutched the edge of his chair and felt his real body beginning to sweat. "Now," she continued, "what is your problem with these beautiful creatures?"

"I guess I've just always been afraid of them. Such depths they live at. They give me a terrible, irrational worry that there's something far bigger than us waiting out there."

"What an odd thing to concern you, a regular traveller outside of the Earth's remit."

"Yeah, well I'm not proud of it." He shrugged. "Just one of those things."

"Maybe it's not really the creatures under the *ocean*'s surface you're afraid of."

"What are you, a psychiatrist now?"

"My mother always told me people are like stars. They have a light inside, and you can tell if something's amiss by the way they shine. In your case, a particular star from a particular constellation. Have you heard of Mira?"

Aaron shook his head.

"Mira is a red giant. It puzzled astronomers when they first spotted it because, as seen from Earth, it had wild variances in luminosity. It's a pulsing star, expanding and contracting. There is a fusion going on at its core, and it's losing mass. The outflow of it can be seen by those with the correct equipment. It's like the tail of a comet, leading to a white dwarf that orbits it."

"Why are you telling me this? That's nothing like me. I'm not losing mass, and I definitely don't have a white dwarf about my person."

"Don't think of the star as your body, think of it as your mind."

"You're bonkers, lady." The door to the restaurant appeared to be working again as several newcomers were now filing in, so Aaron stood to leave. Georgie reached out for his arm as if to pull him back into his seat. The signal was weak. Whoever played this part wasn't in the same building.

"Mira is part of the constellation Cetus. The Sea Monster," she said. Aaron stopped. "Can't you feel it, Aaron? The darkness inside trying to claw its way through you, leaching your energy and brain space?"

He remembered his dream and shuddered. "What do you know about that?"

"A damn sight more than you, it would seem." She poured herself another glass of champagne. "I'm here to help you remember what you did up there."

"What I – did?"

Slow-paced drumming started in the background. It made the walls vibrate in time with the thumping now present in Aaron's head.

"I think, if you search deep inside yourself, you know what really happened up there today," she said. "Now, focus on the drumming please, and take yourself back to evening twenty-three on the station. What were you doing?"

"Evening twenty-three. I would have been checking on the growth of the new Product batch. Preparing to add another round of microbes."

"Is that an important step?"

"We have to make sure we collect the microbes at the right time, yes. The shapes they form when cultivated in low gravity are vital to the beneficial features in Product. Why do you care?"

"Product may be a godsend for human health, but the rumour is its mutated shadow side is the Devil incarnate. It will eat us from the inside, causing all our vital organs to fail. Then, when we are weak enough, it will rip us apart from our bodies and thrust us into an ethereal dimension. The same phenomenon has been appearing across the many worlds in one form or another, wherever it is given the opportunity to penetrate our atmosphere. But then, at least on some level, I think you know that too."

"The *many worlds*? That's just a theoretical model."

"Just focus on the drumming, Aaron."

He began to feel dizzy. He wanted out of the game, out of the warehouse, to get some air. But he was stuck to the spot. Images of the virtual restaurant merged with images of the great squid in the sky, which in turn merged with the great squid in his dreams. He saw his hands folding a great squid out of paper. The same hands that stuffed the package for RJ Quinn with contraband Product. The same hands that packaged up the Product for the home journey after harvesting it and checking it under the microscope. Great squid, he was dizzy.

"Did you check the Product you were bringing home?" Georgie asked. Her voice echoed, as though she was in a tunnel. The drumbeats were getting louder. He saw himself looking through the microscope. Mutated microbes that looked like hyper-pyramids wriggled in the dish, multiplying before his eyes in a thick gel. He took a swab and zipped it up in a plastic bag. Then another and another. He spread the rest onto the Product grow bags and cleaned the dish out with a cloth from his pocket. As though she saw his thoughts, Georgie continued with her questioning.

"And what did you do with that cloth afterwards?"

"I – stuffed it back into my pocket."

"And then?"

Aaron's eyes widened. "I wiped down the seals with it."

"You wiped down the seals with it. What else did you do?"

"I – polished the docking probe."

"Thus, smearing mutated microbes on a soon-to-be external part of your craft."

"Anything on the outside should be burned up on re-entry, but—"

"But?"

"But these particular microbes are resistant to extreme temperatures. And as gravity increases, so does their multiplication. I don't know how I know that. What are you doing to me?"

"So, they could survive atmosphere re-entry. And the closer they got to the surface of the Earth, the more they would multiply?"

Aaron nodded. "Sure. But none of that can have happened. Ground Control would have notified the crew if there was any suspicious activity."

"Ah, but you 'fixed' the cameras, I'm sure?"

Aaron was horrified. "I wouldn't have done that,"

he said, making two fists. "I wouldn't have done that."
Then, at Georgie's request, he recounted his experience
on the return to Earth. All the while, he felt as though he
were about to vomit. His insides were churning, but still
the drums pounded. Still his blood vessels throbbed.

"I'm afraid you're fading, Aaron. So now, if you will
help me, I'd like to speak with the imposter folded into
the gaps of your mind."

"The wha—"

Aaron felt himself pushed into the background of
his own mind. Another consciousness surged forward:
a character who seemed all too familiar. As it settled
into the groove, Aaron felt as though he was watching
his own life from backstage. His body was moving, the
avatar in the game was moving, but it was no longer he
who controlled it. He tried to cry out, but no sound came.
Tried to punch at the glass table, but was paralysed. He
watched his virtual self morphing into a new avatar.
A pointed hat bent over at the top. A beard, long black
braids and a pierced nose.

"Hello Demari," Georgie said.

"Procyon. You found me."

"It was nothing. I just look for the pulsing stars, they all
have their secrets. In this case, a symbiotic white dwarf."

"Who are you calling a white dwarf? I'm a black
magician, I'll have you know."

"You're a degenerate with no energy of his own. Give
me one reason why I shouldn't feed you to the sharks."

"I'll give you three. One: dying in VR does not mean

dying in real life. Trust me on that; I know. Two: dying in real life does not mean dying in real life. You'll just let me slip through your fingers and into another world. And three: you want to hear my story, don't you?" Aaron's body leaned back in the chair. He plucked a brass coin from his palm and rolled it across his knuckles. Aaron himself watched from an unconscious tunnel. "You and I are not so different, Procyon. Both of us have jumped dimensions, crossed worlds, lived many lives by proxy. You must know as well as I that, ultimately, there's no meaning. There's no God. There are no angels. There's no plan. Everything just goes around in circles. It's the same thing in a different flavour, again and again and again. We're forever chasing our own tails. If there's no end to suffering on this level, we must go higher. We have to lose our physical form and go mental."

"My fate has brought my path upon me," said Georgie. "My genes remembered the ways of my ancestors, and so yes, I can travel. But I am not like you. I love life. You are about to destroy all of humanity."

"I'm not destroying it, I'm making it transcend. I'm immanentising the Eschaton! Physicality is so last century. What we need is pure consciousness. Unbridled lust and war. What's the use of having blood if you aren't whipping it up once in a while? Get rid of it."

"And that's what you're achieving with this—"

"Aether virus. Do you like it? It will pull the mind away from the rotting meat sack without the host having to do a thing. I folded up the instructions real small. Hid them inside the genomes, just like I did with Product. Product was supposed to give people the tools to make themselves transcend. But no one can be bothered. They'd rather use abusive quantities and bumble around the bottom of the pyramid, never experiencing much of anything."

Georgie called the waiter over and covered a whisper with her hand. He gulped, nodded, then walked briskly towards the kitchen, almost dropping his silver tray in the process. In the doorway, his avatar dissolved. Aaron, trapped in his tunnel, could see and hear everything, but he could feel only a stabbing pain in his invisible heart.

"How exactly do you travel, anyway, Demari?" said Georgie.

I know what you're doing, Aaron thought. *You're buying time. You have a plan.*

"You've heard of origami? Well the mind, like paper, can be folded. First, you have to flatten it using focus, meditation, drugs. Get all the creases out. That's the part I used to teach, back in the day when I had a body of my own. If you do this having ingested a proper dose of Product, you will begin to see the other worlds. You can skate the probabilities and return with relative ease. Or you can jump right through and perform the fold to squeeze through the gaps in someone else's mind. From there, you can unfold and take over the driving seat of the brain whenever you want. Choose a useful pair of hands for that, would be my advice. The thing to remember is that the mind is still the mind, just as an origami squid is still a piece of paper."

"I knew it. You manipulated an innocent to make the Devil's Product for you. And another to attempt to open a black hole right here on Earth? I can't imagine what you thought you were doing with that one."

"Well, I guess I can tell you now that everything's already in motion. Because my microbes are highly sensitive to gravity for reproduction, I can create tiny black holes to guide their path, should they miss a spot. My servitor will have left the memory stick in the agreed place by now, if it worked."

Aaron's pain ceased abruptly at that moment, but there was no time to feel relief: the landscape was changing. Everything looked ghostly, as though he were looking at it through a veil. He tried desperately to punch his way out of the little squares that now contained him, but they were solid.

"Aaron says he saw a sea monster up there, and a tattooed woman. Are you shapeshifting as well now?"

"The microbes start to multiply rapidly around the Karman line and filter through to the dimensions we perceive. In a hypnogogic state, the brain is more sensitive to such changes and will try to reconcile the stir with something visual it can recognise. Usually something it associates with the triggered emotion. Fear: sea monster. Hope: irrational, unhinged woman who can save the day or inadvertently kill you. Makes perfect sense. Anyway, as delightful as this has been, I should probably be going now. I have a mental kingdom to address."

"Oh, you can't leave, Demari. I'm afraid I've caught the great sea monster in a silicon net."

Demari screwed up his eyes and crossed his arms over his chest. He began to writhe.

"My host! My host is dead."

Dead!

"And yet you're still here. Curious. Maybe you do need a body, after all."

"I can easily migrate, except – you must be hiding all the other bodies from me!"

"There are no other bodies in here, Demari. I am but a copy. Procyon B. A white dwarf orbiting a living star, just like you. I had everyone else evacuated. You're out of luck. Unless, of course, a digital body can somehow meld itself to you. Do you know anyone who might specialise in that sort of thing? Anyone who might know exactly which avatar you'd choose and rig it up in advance?"

"You little bitch!"

"Dog, actually, not that it matters much. The thing about digital bodies," she continued, "is you have to keep a backup. Do you happen to have a backup, Demari?"

Demari stood, grabbed the back of his chair in both hands and threw it at the aquarium wall. Fake glasses and crockery smashed on the floor as he struck them with his fists again and again.

"Oh dear. Perhaps feeding you to the sharks was not such a crazy suggestion after all. Time to shut this place down." That was the last thing she said before she started reciting a long piece of code, and the graphics turned to fuzzy grey pixels one object at a time.

It's all in the fold. Aaron remembered it now. All those times he'd been confined to the back of his own mind, paralysed and unable to act, he'd witnessed Demari performing it. The question was, could he reproduce it? He'd had no training. But he also had no choice.

Listen to the drumbeat.

Thump thump.

Flatten the mind.

Thump thump.

The mind is still the mind.

Thump thump.

The mind is always the mind.

Aaron silenced the chatter in his head, declared the physical to be an illusion and believed it. He let go of his mental attachments and expanded himself beyond them, bursting out of the little boxes on all sides. He cut loose from the MMO just as the furious Demari avatar folded in on itself. Wiped, never to be revived. Aaron was confronted, then, with the sight of his former self: a stiff, non-responsive shell on the warehouse floor. There was no going back now. What the aether virus had brought was something truly alien. Already it would be getting distributed as Product and reproducing worldwide inside our breathable atmosphere. If mind and matter belonged together as a coherent whole, what on Earth would an antidote to detachment look like? He supposed that if the microbes were programmed to purge matter from mind, perhaps an antidote would *create* matter from the mind. He would have to follow Demari's lead and jump into other worlds to find the answer. Use the fold. But there was so little time.

Across the desert he flew, with a cloud of terrified, skittish souls at his tail. He flew over the air ambulance as two men carried Cathy's convulsing body aboard on a stretcher. He flew over the homes of Jermaine and Buddy, each with a medic on their doorstep. He flew over the health centre where the psychologist and the aides were making calls for emergency repatriation. And he set about the search for a host with the skills to make this all go away.

X

"Hold on. Is it right, what we're doing?" he asks.

She shrugs. "It is what it is."

"Don't you have a conscience?"

"Conscience? No. I'm like gravity. Sometimes I help, sometimes I hinder. It just depends on what you are trying to do."

"But you've gone out of your way to help me. And you did say you have something to rectify."

"Oh, that. That's a complicated matter. Circular. Paradoxical, you might say."

"And you can definitely get me out again?"

"A grouping of ideas – that is, you – can hold its shape only while it is in orbit. It can, however, change what it is orbiting around. You'll find I have quite a strong pull when I want to."

Zane decides he should take that as a 'yes'.

HUMANITY V1.1

You have one new message.

"Robyn, it's Pippa. Sorry to ask, but I don't suppose you could come back in? Jen's called in sick. Just one more shift, I promise."

Message deleted.

Robyn let her head hit the steering wheel.

Every time she thought she'd escaped the black hole of perpetual double shifts, they pulled her back in. Not this time. She was exhausted. She wanted a hot dinner, a shower and a snuggle with her wife. Was that too much to ask? Stuck on the A64 for half an hour, moving at a snail's pace, was far from ideal. She sent a text home: *There must have been an accident. Back soon.* The words looked weird on the screen. More like hieroglyphs than letters.

"You're not supposed to be here, you know," a tiny grey man with folded arms scolded from the dashboard. Robyn jerked in shock and the car followed suit, its engine stalling. Her phone clattered to the floor.

"Are you coming with me, then?"

"What?"

The tiny man rolled his eyes. "Ah. You haven't seen my kind before, have you? Came here by accident, I suppose? Well, it's easily done when you're on your way out. We practically occupy the same space, after all."

"On my way out where? I'm on my way home. Looks like I'll be stopping by the lunatic asylum. Why am I talking to a hallucination?"

"Because it's only polite to reply when it talks to you."

"That's it. I've finally cracked up. I knew lack of sleep would be the death of me." Without restarting the engine, Robyn tossed her head back onto the rest closed her eyes. The tiny man began to tap his foot impatiently.

"But I am *not* a hallucination. You prototypes have a funny idea of what constitutes reality."

"Prototypes?"

The tiny man sighed. "The Great Omniscient Darkness moulded you out of the chaos to carry out an important mission, but you failed the willpower test. You've heard of the garden of Eden, right? The snake, the forbidden fruit? Well, that was your factory acceptance test, and you failed. The G.O.D. made your ego too potent. So, it sealed you up in a dimension of physical limitations to breed and run your course where you couldn't interfere with the next version, i.e. us."

The tiny man sat down, dangling his legs over the edge of the dashboard. His eyes were brighter, as though what had first been a drag to explain was now entertaining.

"We were made with larger ears so we might listen more closely to the G.O.D.'s music. We were made smaller so we might see how much we still have to grow. And we were made stronger and smarter so that we might have a fighting chance at understanding our mission. But, we too fell for the lure of good and evil; of believing in right and wrong."

"You ate the fruit?" Robyn was vaguely annoyed with herself for going along with this, but she had been bored in traffic for too long. She yawned.

"The issue was not the eating of the forbidden fruit, for either of us; rather, it was the feeling of shame that followed. That's what created morality and that, in turn, is what made hierarchy implicit in us. That's what complicated and fractured the nature of both 1.0 and 1.1 beyond repair. I like to think that if we had passed, we would all have free will and be successful replicas of the G.O.D. Instead, we live like abandoned, smashed up toys in the attic. We, version 1.1, got sealed in a dimension on top of yours, bound by almost the same laws."

"Almost?"

"We can sometimes find ways to permeate the layers; you can't. Well, not usually, anyway."

"But I haven't moved layers. I mean, literally, I haven't moved at all for forty-five minutes." Robyn looked up to find that, ironically, the traffic had just started to move. She restarted the engine.

"I assume you're here to help the cause," the little grey man continued. "Some of us may still possess the means to find our way out, though we are limited by lifespans of a hundred years before we are recycled. At that point, we lose all memories from before. We have to leave messages behind to remind ourselves. Maybe working with our neighbours, even earlier prototypes, we can find our way through the labyrinth together to prove our willpower."

"Well, I'm glad that's clear," Robyn remarked with sarcasm.

"We can see echoes of the real mission in our world. Bizarre weather patterns, random chaotic events that don't fit with our laws, UFOs…"

The road Robyn was on seemed endless. She drove this stretch daily and could swear it was never so long before. Nor was there any sign of the incident that had held her up. Then she saw it. A green Passat on its roof. *Her* green Passat on its roof.

"So, are you coming with me or what? I'll pull you through. Heba's got a little cottage in the woods over there. She's deaf, but she can still hear you through the hairs on her arms. She'll just need to shift your temporal lobe a bit more. She can do it with a tiny metal stick. Then you can help us find the next black hole that leads to version 1.2."

"How many layers are there?"

"No idea. You coming?"

Robyn stared at her car as she approached. There was an ambulance beside it, with two paramedics leaning over a person on a stretcher.

"What? No, I'm not coming with you! I can't indulge in stupid hallucinations: I've got things to do with my life that don't include being committed to an institution. I'm content with my willpower. Go back to Elfland."

"Elfland?" said a paramedic.

"She's back with us!" called another.

"Can you tell us your name?"

"What's going on? Where am I? Has the Elf man gone?"

"OK, try not to get distressed. You've been in a car accident, you have a head injury, but you're going to be just fine. We're taking you to hospital." A kind face with shining purple eyes reassured her as she and her partner lifted the stretcher into the back of the ambulance.

XI

Zane tries to gulp away his concerns.

"As above, so below," she says. "As the black hole absorbs matter and builds density, so the man sucks in sensory experience and makes the heart heavy." She puts a hand on each of his shoulders. "You have some pieces of the G.O.D. inside you, too. Fractals! All the ideas that have attached themselves to you are spinning around the event horizon of your unconscious. At the centre is your death. You can feel its pull if you concentrate, full of doom and existential despair..." She stops mid-thought in a fit of giggles, slaps her thigh, and wipes a tear from her eye.

"What's so funny?"

"Oh, I'm sorry. It's just your face! Why must you take death so solemnly? There isn't a thing you can do about it. It's bigger than the both of us! I've never understood why you'd want to be in a permanent state, anyway."

FRANKIE

He was a meme artist when I met him, standing on a box in St Helen's Square making images in the sky. A plastic woman with a bionic eye dancing a slow, rhythmic salsa was the first one I saw. I sipped coffee from a paper cup and posed myself in front of him to stream the view to my channel. Some said it was all about having the latest version of Squid, but I thought it was a talent. It needed tremendous willpower to make mind imagery stand still like that, unaffected by the whims of passers-by. He had admirable insight into the underlying patterns of our existence; into understanding and translating the zeitgeist of the generation.

"Nice work!" I told him. He didn't break his concentration but sent a 'thumbs up' impression in my direction. Squid added love hearts to his image on my feed, detecting signals in my subconscious I hadn't registered. I sank into my coffee when I saw them, and my embarrassment bled out like turquoise paint onto the pavement. I could only hope the orange splashes of joy coming from other headsets would be enough to obscure it.

"Michel," he said, holding out his hand to shake mine once the crowd had begun to disperse. "My memes stop people from feeling lonely in their subjective passing through life. I want to say to them all: it's OK, I feel it too! We are not so different, you and I." He tipped his head to one side as if considering me from another angle. I wanted to tell him I didn't feel lonely, that Squid made us part of an elaborate meta-creation, connecting our thoughts and emotions in more ways than ever. But, before I could formulate the words, he added, "I can tell you all about it if you'll let me take you for lunch sometime? I'm here every morning until one, so we could grab something after that? Maybe even today?"

I found his semantics quirky. It was rare for anyone to make plans like that, or even to be in the same place at the same time each day. I agreed to come back at one, and Squid betrayed our enthusiasm in matching clouds of peach.

* * *

"Impermanence leaves me nauseous," he said, stirring sugar into his green tea. "That's how I know it's my calling to create something that will last." We sat outside on aluminium chairs, picking at leafy salads with too much dressing. Most people kept their headsets on even while eating. Despite their rubbery exterior and sucker-like transducers wrapped around the chin, they were cosy and familiar. They made us look like we were hosting futuristic sea creatures, which I suspected was the inspiration for the software name.

"Even memes don't really last, though," I said. "They move around less than ordinary impressions, and they get amplified by the number of people sharing them, but they're far from permanent."

"OK, not permanent, but I think you'd be surprised by their longevity. I'm working hard on my focus. Some of the pieces I've created at home are getting close to being material."

I was instantly taken with the idea he had a home. An actual house, he told me, that was only his. So quaint. Home to me was a state of mind: something that moved around. Squid's projections made any sleep-lodge room feel like an extension of myself, so I never became attached a place.

"I guess I just see everything we create as the motion of love," I said, "between an observer and the observed."

"Yes," he exclaimed, "and that's the very idea we must build on."

The excitement in his eyes, his supple lips. The boldness with which he took my hands in his. All the qualia combined as a tingling sensation in my heart, and sent vivid colours bouncing around the table.

* * *

There was a mat inside the door that said 'Welcome'. Welcome to polished hardwood floors, cluttered shelves and more possessions than I could ever imagine acquiring. Books and gadgets and china pots and trinkets. He had plants, too. Lots of them, all through the house. There was even a conservatory at the back where he grew tomatoes and jasmine in the summertime. A single wicker chair was placed beside them, pointing not towards the bare brick of the main house, which would have made a grand canvas for experimenting with Squid, but looking out of the window at a lawn overrun with weeds.

The first time I visited, he cooked me a beautiful dish of brown rice with black bean, tofu and avocado. He showed me some of the new memes he was working on and tried to give me a crash course in the process: I failed terribly. There was a quietness in the house I had rarely experienced anywhere else, and it made me dream. It uncovered something unknown that was asleep in my unconscious. York was pretty, I thought. Perhaps I could stick around for a while.

When I moved in, we hung a canvas above the bed to represent our shared vision. We held hands and closed our eyes, imagining what our future together might look like. Squid interpreted it as a rising sun peeking out from behind a mighty mountain, highlighting the mist over a still lake. It was a stunning image and in the most favourable colours. We put our headsets into private mode and made love hard and fast beneath it. Fireworks burst across the walls.

"I wish we could stay this way forever," he said after. It was an odd thing to say. Relationships, like life, were fluid, and this whole idea of having a man and a place to go back to every day was going to take some getting used to. "You are the secret ingredient," he said as he kissed my neck, "for all creativity."

He was always awake before me. By the time I rose, he would be knelt on the rug in the front room, wearing loose-fitting black linen, reaching up high to focus his sculpt. There were some images he'd make every morning, which seemed to serve as warm-up exercises. There was a perfect circle, an elaborate sigil, and then a winking face: the woman with the cyborg's eyes. That was a popular one on the streets, but some days she was more defined than others.

We'd exchange a few words, but more commonly we'd share thoughts and feelings on the walls. Then, at nine every morning, he would commute to the square in town. He rode an old-fashioned bicycle with a thin frame and was at his spot with a regularity I already couldn't abide. I would take walks around the city. I liked to go to new places to take in and put out the sights, sharing my Squid feed all the way. This is also the way I earned my credits: new experiences got more views and counted, therefore, as valued content. Credits paid for food, sleep-lodge space and, more importantly for me, travel to new locations.

Even in the afternoons, Michel wouldn't come exploring with me. He said that time spent augmenting the present was time stolen from pondering the past and making plans for the future. He said indulging in fleeting

203

fancies was illusory, and wounded his art; that it caused him to lose focus on his goals and high-level thinking. So, when he wasn't at the square, he was quietly creating floating images of strange pot plants, mirrors and eyes without faces. He spent more time working on them than he did with me, though he swore my presence was somehow helping them to thrive.

Perhaps I should have known, then, that something subversive had its hooks in me. Perhaps I should have seen that he never wanted to be a functional part of the whole. He preferred to look from the outside and study the rest of us. He rowed against the current. While the depth we could put into the space around us was ever expanding and evolving through the medium of metaphysics, he was somehow making these little fixtures. Anchors digging into time he couldn't bear to let go of.

* * *

I named her Frankie. He called her White Lily. She must have come during the night, because it was early morning when I discovered her grotesque form in the closet under the stairs, slumped against an old tumble drier. She wasn't human, that much was clear, but she was wrapped in pale, clammy skin. Instead of having fingers and toes, her limbs tapered at their ends like roots. Her head was without detail. Her chest rose and fell, like someone breathing into a bag. Squid projected my unease as a twisted expression upon her face and deep, dark holes for eyes. A sea-green snake slithered across the walls as I battled with the sickness clawing to get out of me. I slammed the door shut and prayed she'd be gone in the morning.

* * *

We had nothing but rain and fog for a week. It didn't stop Michel making his commute, but I chose to stay inside. I went exploring in the loft and found an old camera, thick with dust. Some of the boxes of film were disintegrated, but others were intact. I took them downstairs and, after a little research, I set up a rudimentary darkroom in the utility cupboard. There wasn't an external window in there, so it was easy to equip it with old sheets, bin bags and trays. I pinned up some string and coloured pegs. Sometimes, if they were particularly beautiful formations, I photographed the impressions Squid made on the back wall of the conservatory. More interesting were the natural subjects. What I loved most about them was the way they looked during the process of developing a film. Watching their images morphing through various stages of beauty and representation. Once they reached their conclusion and depicted a flat, unchanging reality, I was no longer so thrilled by them. I tossed most away. Michel said a photograph was a wonderful thing because it captured the very soul of something and allowed it to live on beyond its usual means. It wasn't so different from meme art, he said. It was all part of the immortalisation of feelings and moments. Memes spread like viruses to stay alive, though. Photographs were souls captured in matter itself. The very idea made me shudder, and I packed the camera away.

I started leaving food out for Frankie. I didn't know what else to do. She wouldn't eat in front of me, but if I left a bowl with her for a few hours, it was usually empty when I returned. Porridge was her favourite; that always went the quickest, but she'd also accept unsweetened rice pudding. Sometimes she just wanted a saucer of milk. Her body would jerk around afterwards, using the energy to perform some kind of dance from outer space. I don't know if Michel was feeding her too. We rarely spoke about Frankie. By that point, we rarely spoke at all.

Our canvas had come to depict a stormy sky. A hooded figure who had appeared on the lake below was struggling to keep control of his rowboat. The omens echoed from our subconscious right there in front of us, and yet we didn't talk it through. We just let those dark clouds become heavier and heavier.

The bathroom was my space without Squid, where I would inspect my underlying baldness and massage it clean. When Michel left for work, I would lie motionless in cloudy bath water for an hour or more, trying to imagine what it would be like to exist with no understanding of the world, no consciousness, and no software to translate sensory data. To be isolated from a system most took for granted. With such imaginings came a pull towards an obscure, unknown force residing within me. It was an emotion born of impending doom and eternal longing; something that didn't speak any language of this world and knew no form or colour. It was an unconscious compulsion with sharp teeth, nibbling at pieces of me that never were. I never allowed myself to acknowledge such thoughts when I wore my headset. Part of me feared what they would look like if I did. What they wanted. What they would create.

As I got used to Frankie being there and understood that she was absorbing nutrients in her own way, her expression progressed to nonplus. Deep indigo flourished in her eyes, and her thin lips made an O shape.

"She has your eyes," Michel said one morning. His words startled me for he said so few. "White Lily, I mean. She has your eyes." He went back to his work.

* * *

Autumn rain with splashes of colour from the leaves and emotions shining through was a beautiful sight. Nature turns yellow and orange in the autumn, which would be interpreted as happiness if it were human, yet droves of us come out in blues once the sun is hidden away. The bleak, uncommunicative atmosphere of Michel's house spilt into the outside, using me as a medium. My thoughts tainted the communal artwork on the pavement as I walked; the cold colours of grief and despair were unwelcome blemishes. *Why does no one find sadness beautiful?* I wondered.

"You should go to the abyss," one woman suggested. On some level she was trying to be helpful, but her condescension and disgust showed in pale pink on the stones at her feet. She pulled up a map and pointed to a small black circle to the North-East of the city, a little way past the laboratories. "You can get a bus. The demand out there is rising." Her last statement seemed loaded with contempt, but I ignored it, and Squid did too. I thanked her and began walking.

The abyss was an area untouched by man and his technology: a flat field with a solid circle of rocks at the centre and several lone commuters stooping around the edges. Squid dressed each of them in a hooded cloak and pixelated their sombre, sobbing faces. I joined them daily, to kneel on the damp grass and pour my despair upon the rocks.

With repeated visits, sadness and confusion made a pit of that rocky ground. The abyss became a theoretical mass of thought eroded deep into the earth, like a gap in the programming. All the disconnection, the unspoken words and the uncertainty could be poured away there. But it was the dark longing in our minds, I believe, that began to move the mental sludge into a swirling vortex, which could not only be seen but heard. It sang, at first, like a finger circling crystal glass. Later it howled, and we wept still more at the shock of its vibrations upon our bodies. Our tears were absorbed instantly by the dissonance of the marvellous mixture.

* * *

Back at the house, more and more of my living environment was becoming blocky and rigid. Michel had turned into a medium for the material, channelling objective, sluggish versions of reality. Boxes, tables, trees and lumps of metal, all placed on top of one another. Every new creation he presented seemed to be on a different frequency that I couldn't quite reach: another dimension lying beneath ours, perhaps, that was sludgy and blubbery and stale. As I couldn't project onto them, I couldn't understand his objects in terms of me and my relationship to them.

I didn't tell him how I felt. I didn't tell him about the abyss, or the void that was building within me. I didn't tell him that Frankie was becoming more like a person every day and that it scared me beyond measure. It is in human nature to keep secrets, I think. What makes us smart is also what allows us to choose between keeping an idea inside and sharing it. But the things we hide from ourselves – and from Squid, even when we are alone – can become monstrous. They can lurk in surprising places, and they can strike.

* * *

I went to see him performing as a surprise one morning. It was cold outside, so I made him a thermos of tomato and basil soup, foolishly thinking it might act as an olive branch. As I approached the square at 12.30, I saw he had a new meme in his repertoire. One of a woman, an apparent hybrid of Frankie and me, kneeling down and sobbing by the abyss. He'd created a separate image that he controlled at the same time, that appeared as though it was behind her back. A big juicy red apple. Everyone was streaming it and laughing. I didn't understand. The joke was beyond me and yet somehow about me. My anger and hurt exploded onto the pavement, pushing its way to him in ripples. He lost concentration, and the images broke apart. I threw the thermos at him and ran back to the house.

Later, when he found me in the kitchen, piecing together my torn photographs into something new, he banged his fist down hard on the table. "You are chaos, do you know that? You're in a permanently excitable state, and it's making me nauseous. I tried to bring you some stability, but if you won't accept my gifts, then what can I do?"

The walls started to turn blue as tears welled up in my throat.

"Where is the girl who stays solid and faithful and quiet and happy? And you can take that thing off as well, if you're not going to use it properly." He reached over and yanked at Squid. My input to the décor wobbled and fuzzed. "You are not turning out the way I imagined."

I clung to Squid, thwarting his attempt to disconnect me, and slowly rose from the table. My eyes rested on his long enough for the hearts around his face to start breaking in two, then I ran to the bathroom and locked the door behind me.

I didn't remove Squid. I just lay, hugging my knees and watching as the blueness bled right into the corners of the room like ink on blotting paper. It was getting darker.

Time passed. I couldn't say how much. I rose to my feet and looked in the mirror at my crow's feet and pale skin. My mouth open, my eye sockets emptied and became swirling holes like the abyss. I knew what I had to do.

I listened at the door for Michel but heard nothing. I slid the lock across as discreetly as possible and cringed as the door creaked open. Creeping down the hallway, I could see he was on his mat, focusing intensely on his images as though our conversation had no bearing whatsoever.

She had an apple core by her side. Her eyes had turned from indigo to an eerie violet, pin-prick black holes forming at their centres, and she was looking up at me. I set her down on her feet, and she stood rigid like a mannequin: her knees bent and together, her feet facing one another, her head drooped down to her chest. "Can you walk, Frankie? At least try?" There was no response. I hitched her up onto my shoulder and carried her out of the house, being careful not to disturb Michel or any of his creations on the way.

We made our way through the streets. People stopped to stare. "What is she? A new kind of meme? I've never seen anything like it!" Their comments confirmed she was indeed a universal construct, a vision of a person that was objectively true. But I couldn't stop now.

* * *

The abyss had begun to rumble constantly. Its smell had become almost noxious, but it was teeming with new participants nevertheless. Vibrations nuzzled into my bones from some distance away as though they would hook me and pull me right in. We reached our destination quicker than I expected, as the circumference was now far wider than it once was. It sprawled outwards on all sides, perhaps by miles. Our great depression would devour all in its path, and soon it would reach the city's edge, whether the conformists liked it or not.

After walking so briskly with Frankie's awkward mass upon me, I was exhausted and thirsty. A wave of relief passed over me as I could finally put her down, and we dropped to the ground in a heap. I drank readily from a bottle of water.

Frankie was, as ever, unmoving. But then I noticed her face. It had changed again. My heart pounded to escape the prison of my ribcage, and I could barely catch my breath as I rummaged in my bag for my hand mirror. When I found it, I turned it to take a selfie of the two of us, and Squid confirmed my suspicions. Our two faces were identical. When my expression changed to one of horror, so too did hers. I saw it now. I saw the whole picture that had been developing since I arrived in York. And now it was time we both got as far away as we could. I'd be OK, I had plenty of credits saved up and no possessions to take care of. Well, only one.

"Don't be scared," I told her. "You're not meant for this world. They'll take care of you on the other side." I gathered all my strength, physical and emotional alike. Then, with one big shove, I gave her to the abyss.

* * *

Beauty is transient. We can pick a tulip and put it in a vase. We can put a cloche over it. But we can't preserve its beauty. Beauty is a moment, a perception, a feeling inside. A quale. It is a love born by observing and responding. When the physical form dries up, we store its impression in our memory: the flower press of the mind. A unique, flatter version of it lives on within anyone who witnessed it. And from there, with that fabulous neural network of ours that both remembers the past and imagines the future, we can forge our own beauty. A different version of you exists in the mind of everyone who has met you. And maybe that's where they should stay.

XII

"But you do understand why I want to rebuild the human race in my own world?"

"I can imagine. There is one thing you should consider, though, if you want this to be a success. All of these consciousness uploads: they'll all remember their pasts, but come from different realities. In most cases, their memories will conflict. They'll either get labelled as fictions or cause a war, if you're not careful."

"I believe they will converge, for the sake of progress."

M raises an eyebrow. "They will not all have the same starting assumptions. There are huge differences from tribe to tribe, world to world. Someone has to establish the assumptions for all, or you'll have anarchy. Don't get me wrong, I love a bit of anarchy. I'm just warning you. Bear it in mind when you pick."

"M?" He looks straight into her vibrant purple eyes with his own, and squeezes her hand. "Thanks."

THE LAST MAN

"More tea, Sir?"

"Yes please, it's wonderful. Is it a local leaf?"

"Oh no, we don't grow leaves of this quality in the labs. This is freshly picked and teleported from India. Only the best on the Timeless Express."

The waitress, in her freshly steamed uniform, poured from a height with great skill. The sun's rays beat down on the pink and yellow fondant fancies she had brought on her tray, and the children squealed their delight on noticing them. Zane beamed with pride.

"Take all you like, kids. We can live a life of luxury now Daddy has a job in the city."

Their mum cast him a sideways glance as if to say 'just this once, don't go spoiling them' but there was a glint of excitement there for her, too. She could always express so much with those deep hazel eyes, and Zane loved her all the more for it. He gave her hand a squeeze beneath the table.

"When will we be there, Daddy?" Tiffany asked, her face already covered in cake crumbs and icing. "I can't wait to see all those tall buildings!"

"Yeah!" Chirped Benjamin. "I wanna ride the elevator right to the top!"

"Not long to wait now, the Express is very fast. Keep looking out of the window, and soon you'll spot the tallest one there is."

Zane pulled a photograph from the pocket of his crisp, tailored suit jacket. "Here, this is it. And this one behind it – that's where Daddy's going to work." The kids had seen the photo many times leading up to their journey, but they were still in awe every time.

"Daddy's going to be an Organic Laboratory Technician," Tiffany told her little brother in the matter-of-fact tone she'd learned from her mother. "That means he grows kidneys and eyes and hearts."

"I can see it I can see it I can see it!" Benjamin stood up and pointed out of the window. Zane felt a warm buzz in his chest. Then another, then another. But the tear of joy that had formed in his eye quickly turned into a shard of despair as the scene before him began to disintegrate.

"We will shortly be arriving in the City of Greater York. Passengers are advised to turn off all headsets and prepare to disembark."

He tried to reach out to the children as they faded before him, but there was nothing there to cling to. The cakes, the tea, the waitress, were no more. His wife, long gone. As his visor became transparent, the glorious sunshine pouring over luscious green fields became the same desolate, barren grey that now covered every part of the country Zane was still able to explore. The single tear dripped inside his self-contained respiration helmet as he pulled out the cable. He made a fist with a gloved hand, barely willing to accept that his morning commute was already over. His little act of escapism seemed to go quicker every day. But then, time was a curious thing to a lonely man. Memories and naive hopes for the future all took on a hazy, nostalgic quality that could easily be one or one hundred years past.

The train, an automatic solar-powered engine and a single carriage, slowed to a stop in the station. This was not Greater York proper, but the biomedical technology village on the outskirts. Zane had worked there before the virus hit, and he continued to do so even now. Something deep inside told him it was the only thing he *could* do.

Stepping out onto the platform, he looked up to the sky. By the lack of sunlight getting through the clouds, he estimated it could be a couple of days before the train had enough power to take him home again. He was used to staying over at the lab, though. It was probably the safer thing to do, even, but the commute from his carefully sealed home had become a ritual. It was a way to maintain some semblance of normality; a reassurance there was somewhere he belonged.

Just as he was about to turn away, something else caught his attention in the sky. Something small and dark, and moving fast. Over the past few months, it had become common to see glowing pieces of satellites falling against the backdrop of the night sky. Abandon all hope, they told Zane, the people are gone, and they aren't coming back. But in the daytime, they couldn't be seen, especially on such a cloudy day. Perhaps the sky itself was finally falling in, then. He shuffled off towards the laboratory, the thick plastic of his suit crinkling as he walked.

Like teleporting tea, the 'organ factory' was someone's half-imagined idea of a future that never came. The artificial meat they grew was as widespread as hyper-realistic VR, but creating functioning human parts was – en masse, at least – a failed enterprise. Zane personally witnessed many attempts, and there were some success stories among them, but when the virus hit they were nowhere close to meeting demand for new hearts. It took days to grow a full one, and if the immune system were to accept it, it must incorporate an exact DNA match for the host. At the speed the infection spread, there was very little chance of saving anyone but the rich, who had already invested in the development fund and secured their samples. Even they caught it a second time around, though, and there's no coming back from that. Now, years later, the labs that housed such projects were abandoned like everything else. The angular aluminium cladding was discoloured, and the forecourt was overrun with weeds. Zane tried his best, but there was only so much one man could do.

It was dark inside the building, but to avoid overloading the electrics 'no unnecessary lights' was one of his rules. When Eddie was still around, the two of them had set about securing isolated environmental power systems to keep the laboratory running. Eddie had the expertise, but Zane assisted wherever he could. His primary responsibility was the meat: with crops failing and livestock infected, it was their only safe source of fresh food. It was a venture he took seriously even now, growing enough to feed the other survivors just as soon as they arrived.

He wouldn't remove his helmet until he had been through the wind bath. Most people had baulked at the idea of wearing one at all. There was nothing in the air, they'd said. It was only in the food and water supply. But as he watched the virus spreading, fatally in every instance despite the free miracle pills, he wondered how they could be so sure.

Once safely inside the cleanrooms, he unzipped his gloves and unclipped the catches that connected his helmet to his suit. Lifting it off gave a pleasant sensation of being light, but also naked and exposed. He ran his fingers through his sticky hair. Time to eat.

He opened a sealed portion of homegrown meat and placed it under a microscope to check for abnormalities. All fine. He swallowed his multivitamins with bottled water, then poured the rest into a kettle to make black coffee and instant potato. He sat at his desk among the sample racks and looked into the eyes of his late wife, Bonnie. The photograph had been taken in Marbella, two years before the first signs of her sickness. They promised Product would cure her. *They promised*. But it didn't, and he'd refused to touch the stuff ever since. It may have been a godsend for most, but it had betrayed him.

A deafening rumble dragged Zane out of the world in his head. He hoped the power wasn't failing. Eddie had tried his best to leave instructions, but at the end, he had made sense only intermittently. Hallucinations, delirium, profuse sweating. Then, several hours later, organ failure and the acutest pain Zane had ever witnessed a person go through. The tragedy was they could make replacements in hours now, almost any organ. But they had no surgical expertise, and still no cure to make it last. Zane shuddered.

From the window, he could see a big black object falling out of the sky. He looked again through his binoculars but couldn't make out what it was. It could be nothing. But it could be something useful. He sighed. It looked as though the helmet was going back on already.

* * *

He trundled along the dirt path, pulling his handcart of tools and spare oxygen. The object was further away than he'd thought. Field after footpath after farm road he passed. And then he saw it. A black orb the size of a double-decker bus, laying on the ground. It looked like a giant apple, though its skin appeared to be made from a curious hybrid of rubber and metal. Zane edged closer. The surface was smooth, except for a bumpy square plate on the underside. He ran his fingers along the line that separated it from the rest of the object. He felt sure he should leave it alone, and yet curiosity was nibbling at his ear. *Take a look inside. What harm can it do?*

With his crowbar, and with considerable effort, he prised the plate open. A strange smell came from within, noxious like gas but sweet like apple pie. The strength of it sent Zane reeling backwards. It took him a moment to realise he couldn't usually smell anything when wearing his helmet. Something was wrong. Frantically, he fumbled with the clasps and zips to check they were all secure.

Beneath his feet, the ground was sizzling. He gaped at the cracked asphalt around the orb's base. First, it appeared to be darkening. Then it was melting. And then it was difficult to tell if there was anything there at all. Black, bottomless, empty space covered the land where the road once was, and the area affected was slowly creeping outwards in all directions. He pulled his boot away just before it reached him and took a few swift paces back. The edge of the cart, still in the danger line, was dissolving before his eyes. He let go of the handle like it was a hot poker and ran.

* * *

Light-headed and dry, Zane stopped to catch his breath and check on oxygen levels. Still ten minutes from the lab, and the gauge was reading dangerously low. For the first time, he turned to look at the devastation behind him. For several kilometres on all sides of the great black apple, above and below it too, there was simply nothing there. It was like looking into a giant void. It had stopped growing a few metres behind him, but now, emanating from a point within the darkness, was a vibrant purple glow. The more Zane stared into it, the more it took on the appearance of a tunnel and, walking out towards him, was the silhouette of a woman. Surely this must be a mirage. But never before had a mirage been so detailed. As the figure came closer, Zane could make out a skinny, pale frame decorated with colourful tattoos. She wore her hair short and spiky and had dimples that highlighted her beam. She carried a leather jacket in one hand and something too small to make out in the other.

"Hello?" his voice was croaky and muffled through the speakers, which hadn't been used in weeks. As she stepped out of the void and onto the road, he reached out with both arms, trying to expose her form as illusory.

"Congratulations!" she said, letting off a single party popper in his face.

"Huh?"

"I said: Congratulations! As of the present moment, you are the last man in this world. The last human, in fact."

"What? No. That… can't be true. I've not seen another person for a long time, but the world's a big place. Someone will come eventually. You've come…"

"Ah, but I'm not human. I'm M."

He sunk down to his knees and pushed his knuckles into his visor.

"You don't have to look so glum about it. From my observations, that's the endgame for humanity, isn't it? It's what you all strive for. To be the last."

"It really, really isn't."

"Oh." She looked down at her untied army boots as she kicked at loose stones. "Are you sure?"

"Very."

"This is awkward." She gestured with the empty party popper and tossed it over her shoulder. It melted in the void. Her face scrunched up then, as though thinking hard. Zane started as he suddenly remembered his oxygen tank, but to his surprise, the gauge had shot back up to half.

"I suppose," she said, "I could be human. I mean, I may be a little piece of chaos wearing the costume of a woman, but that doesn't necessarily mean I'm less human than you. Does it?"

He ignored her bizarre rhetorical questioning and went for the more burning topic in his mind. "You look so very familiar. If I didn't know it to be impossible, I'd think you were a young Bonnie…"

"You're observing me from a solidly constructed paradigm, so you'll see what you recognise. It's not your fault, you're just conditioned to minimise errors and factors irrelevant to humanity."

Zane's eyes felt like they were about to pop right out of his head. The woman laughed, but without cruelty. He couldn't remember the last time he had heard merriment, and for a moment it quickened his heart. But he was angry, and he was confused.

"And what the fuck is all this?" he gestured at the great black dome in front of him.

"Oh, that. That's just where the data structure is starting to disappear. It was all a code built in your minds, see. A collective tunnel of reality. But one man's signal on its own isn't strong enough to keep it going. I stopped the void spreading any further, so I could come and get you."

"Get me? Where exactly do you expect to go?"

"Into the gaps."

"The gaps. Well, that's just fucking marvellous." He could feel the beads of sweat forming on his forehead. For so long he'd kept his cool, the pretence of normality, the pretence of hope. But this strange woman who wasn't a woman, and this open space that was now *only* a space, was just too much.

"I'm sensing you'd rather have your species back," M said.

Zane threw his hands in the air and began walking again. She trudged behind him, making no effort to keep up with his stride.

Grateful for the relinquished assault of new information, he hadn't questioned the silence at first. But as soon as he sensed she was no longer behind him, he took a tentative glance. She was crouched by the stream, cupping water in two hands.

"No, you mustn't drink that!" he shouted. "That's just for the power."

She curled her lip on one side and drank anyway. "It's OK. Your disease won't affect me."

"If you're really not human, then what are you exactly?"

"There's no time for that now. We can do the small talk once we're in the gaps."

"The gaps again! What are you talking about?"

"The body likes continuity. It's part of the deal. But the truth is, there are gaps everywhere. Gaps in space, gaps in time, gaps in all your theories. Gaps only the mind can slip through."

"Must you speak in riddles?"

"I'm not the one making holes in things, if that's what you mean."

Zane glared at her and turned to walk away again. She reached out to his shoulders, and for the first time, he felt she was as real as him.

"OK, OK. I'm sorry," she said. "I should have explained better. You've heard of the many worlds theory?"

Now this piqued his interest. "Every moment is a fork, and every version of reality is played out in a different parallel world?"

"Right. Well, it's not just a theory. I can take you travelling in the many worlds right now. If you stay here alone, you're going to be swallowed by a void. If you come with me, you can live a life beyond your imagination and see how other branches of team human are faring. Have some fun for a change."

"So, you could take me to a world where the virus

never happened?"

"I could. It wouldn't mean you'd get your life back, though. That's a game for another instance of your consciousness to play."

"What about time travel, can you do that? I want to see my wife and kids again."

"Time travel." She rolled her eyes. "Were the wife and kids really your past, Zane, or were they your future? How can you know for sure? There is only the present."

"What? Wait, you know my name?"

"Well of course I do. What a funny thing to say."

* * *

She accompanied him back to the lab, but he didn't allow her inside the cleanrooms. All this time waiting for some company, and now he needed some time alone, to think.

He unpinned the photograph of him and Bonnie from the board. There was the proof he wasn't going insane. Of course she existed, of course she had been his wife. The strange visitor said a photograph only exists as an affect in the present and we make up the most probable history to explain its being there. But he knew the truth. He'd experienced it. The kids were another matter, though. He had met with them daily on his commute to work, but were there any real memories there? Could he remember what had happened to them, where they had gone? To his horror, he wasn't sure.

A screeching sound came from the next room. She'd

somehow sneaked into the labs without him noticing and, to his disbelief, she'd set the printers going. Several bright red human hearts were dangling from the branches of the plastic tree he'd made, and the gel holding their layers together was in mid-evaporation.

"Look, Zane!" she said. "We can grow you some friends. Isn't that fantastic?"

He flicked off all the machines and sighed. "Being human isn't just about organs and meat. What about mind, what about consciousness?"

"Luckily for you, consciousness is my specialism. I know how to collect copies of minds from any reality."

"You want me to live with *copies* of people?"

"What difference does it make? They'll have seamless continuity, and so will you. I assume you can grow brains on trees too, so we can culture them?"

Zane shook his head. "We never got that far. What use is it anyway, if we don't understand the disease? Everyone would just die all over again." She looked crestfallen. "I'm grateful you tried to help," he said. "Really, I am. It's just no use: we can't build new bodies."

"So, you're going to come with me then?"

"Let me sleep on it. There's a lot I don't understand. Hell, I don't even know if I can trust what you say. I fear my judgement is being clouded by your familiarity. Do you want me to make you a bed up somewhere?"

"It's OK. I don't really sleep. I'll just look around, maybe take a walk."

* * *

He looked out at the night sky. On a clear night, he spent hours staring up at the distant stars, spotting constellations, wondering if there could be life out there. On this night he could think of little else but whether that giant dome of void was creeping out towards the laboratory, and how he would even know if it was already upon him. He shivered violently, though it wasn't cold.

He was willing to believe the many worlds were real. It was a concept used only to illustrate the possibilities on a quantum level, but he was all too aware that everything we call science was once called magic. For years, the same nagging voice inside that told him to boycott Product, stay clean, wear a hazmat suit, make a routine and get the organ printers up to maximum efficiency, was also an advocate of the theory. And this woman – Em – she might be his last chance of happiness. He'd be distraught at leaving his base world, of course, but what options did he have, really?

The clouds had cleared enough over the last couple of hours for him to make out the constellation of the winter triangle. 23 September. Autumn would soon be upon him.

* * *

When he awoke, she was nowhere to be seen. Disappointment weighed heavy in his stomach: perhaps this had all been a dream after all. He took out his binoculars and saw that the void and the giant apple were still there. But something was different. Something had changed within. He put on his suit and helmet and set off on the 2.3km walk to the edge of the dome.

Ground had returned at the base of the void. It wasn't fields or roads like it was before, but a flat plane of solid metal sheeting. A pixelated display was hanging in the ethereal wall that read '*Area under construction*'. Em jumped out at him.

"I've had a beautifully chaotic idea." Her eyes were wild with excitement. "You want to rebuild your race, right, but the human body is not robust enough to weather the virus in your atmosphere?"

"Yes…" he said hesitantly.

"Well, I found this."

"That's a prototype housing for AI."

"Thought as much. Like I said, I can make copies of human consciousness. See where I'm heading with this?"

"Unfortunately, yes I do."

"Why unfortunately? I thought it was my best idea yet."

"If a man believes he is a machine, will he behave like one?"

"You mean with efficiency, speed and focus? I'd say that sounds pretty on point for rebuilding a race, environment and society."

"But such an ugly body to exist in. So artificial and restrictive."

"Ahem." She looked him up and down in his plastic suit and gloves, heavy helmet and visor.

"Fair point. It all sounds very fake, though."

"Whether something is fake or not largely depends on which filter you are choosing to look through at the time. The territory is not the map."

"You mean the map is not the territory."

"It's the same thing, isn't it? I've always thought maps were more interesting than territories. You can do more with an idea than a fact, and more with a mind than you can a brain."

Zane sat down on the grass and thought for a while. "The virus is going to go away eventually without anything to feed on, I get that. It will at least go into torpor. If we can be preserved, we'll outlive it. But the conditions we'll be left with are likely to be favourable for neither man nor machine. We'd have to treat the atmosphere, build everything from the ground up. It's going to take hundreds of years!" He was suddenly overwhelmed by the enormity of the situation, and his voice began to quiver.

She patted him on the back. "There, there. It'll work, I'm sure. The android bodies will increase your endurance. You can program them however you want by building in rules. The status quo is in your hands. You want lifetime loops equal to standard human ones, you got it. You want a continuation of memories to build up in the individual over hundreds of years, you could do that. In fact, I'll take you some places where you can get an idea of what that might look like. I can even take you somewhere this robot dome exists. If you find it unbearable, you can come back into the gaps with me."

"You made ground," he pointed out.

"Yep. It can mimic your laws of physics, too, if you want. The inside of the dome is free from everything unless we choose it. That includes your disease. Look," she reached up to his face and tugged at the mask. He resisted. "Trust me, come on."

"I didn't survive so long by trusting just anything."

"I agree. Anything and everything is suspicious. But you can trust me because I'm nothing."

He didn't move.

"Oh, come on. What does it matter now?"

He allowed her to take his hand and pull him into the dome. Slowly, cautiously, he fumbled with the catches for his helmet and lifted it up high. For the first time in years, he breathed natural air. It was exhilarating. His heart quickened.

"So, what do you want it to look like? I thought we could make this." She produced a crumpled cut-out from one of his VR magazines. It depicted a high-tech futuristic city with tall buildings, artificial weather systems and a sky-train. "You like it?"

"I guess. But how do we get that here?"

She unrolled a sticky transparent screen and used it to attach the image to the wall. He watched it unfold before his eyes, growing outwards by several inches and duplicating buildings as it went. The world within it was becoming 3D. Zane took off his glove and reached right into it. He could hold one of the tiny skyscrapers between forefinger and thumb, but it was already expanding.

"Over time, the sphere at the centre will solidify like black wax. It'll still hold the dome, but its tunnel, and the instruction to absorb, will seal up."

"So, how do we manifest in other worlds? What will we look like, what will we do?"

"Well, I'll look like this. You've pretty much set that with your observations. You'll look however the first human to set eyes on you imagines you to look. As for what we'll do – very little. Things get messy if you interfere too much. Keep your spooky action at a distance, that what I suggest."

"And they won't suspect that we don't belong there?"

She shrugged. "People just seem to accept me as part of their scenes. They'll accept you too, I guarantee it.

"Now, we'll need a fail-safe in case you change your mind and want out. I'll trust you with this." She held up a memory stick with the letter M written on it in permanent marker. "I'll leave it well away from the others, in a box buried in your old back garden. You can plug it into the underside of the sphere for a reboot, or into a computer to open up a hole. You can go travelling, then. Wherever you want."

"But how?"

"I'm coming to that, Zany boy. You see, you're going to come with me to get the uploads and learn the ropes."

* * *

They wandered slowly back to the labs, Zane with his helmet back on once more. They talked all the way. This might well be the worst decision Zane had ever made, but she made him feel something he'd have no hope of feeling again should he stay. She was chaotic, energetic and at times utterly insane. But she lit a fire in his mind and heart that he'd forgotten he had.

He ran through his cleanroom routine for the last time, removed his protective gear, and sat down at his desk.

"I'll transfer you into data format using one of these," she said, holding up a black box with a bunch of wires hanging out. "You won't feel a thing; it'll be really smooth. You'll be out for a little while until we're safely curled up in the gaps. I'll make a couple of checks, adjustments. Bury the copy of me, bury the bones of you. But you won't feel as though any time has passed. It'll just be like you're suddenly seeing through a new set of eyes."

"Will it still be me, though? How is it any different to the versions living in split-off worlds?"

"You'll have continuity. You won't be a copy, you'll just be migrated. Now, what's your favourite song?"

Zane hadn't thought about music in a long time. "I don't know. I suppose – 'The Passenger'?"

"Hum it."

"Really? Do I have to?"

"Hum it. There's an old myth that it will keep your mind in one piece as you travel."

"We're dealing with myths, now? I thought this was scientifically sound?"

"What on earth gave you that impression? You won't get far with rationality alone."

Zane started humming. If nothing else, it would stop him thinking too hard about what the flux he was actually doing.

"The upload will take around ten minutes. If you still care about time, that is. Then we'll go get the rest."

!

"Ready?"

AUTHOR'S NOTE

Never content with something straightforward, I wanted to create stories that are individually entertaining and though-provoking, but collectively reminiscent of a many-faceted reality; the truth cannot be found in any one story we tell ourselves, only in the whole collection. I doubt whether the un-enhanced human brain has the capacity to perceive the complete picture of our world, so we have to make do with fragments: one-off Polaroid shots at single moments in space and time. We fill the gaps only with expectation and speculation. But that will never stop us from making a puzzle of it all, and therein lies the nature of being human, I think. *Mind in the Gap*, therefore, is layered and full of inter-connections, possible causes, and Easter eggs. How many did you spot?

CONNECT

Did you enjoy the book? Please consider leaving a review on your favourite bookstore's website or social media pages.

For Mind in the Gap discussion and extras, head over to www.orchidslantern.com. If you'd like to receive updates and new flash fiction straight to your inbox, you can also join the mailing list there.

You can connect with the author via:

Twitter: @orchidslantern
Instagram: orchidslantern
Facebook: www.facebook.com/orchidslantern

ACKNOWLEDGEMENTS

Writing a book is only the beginning; publishing it is a team effort.

First and foremost I'd like to thank my husband, Cy, who offers an immense amount of patience while I talk ideas through and try to get every scene right. He is always my first reader and has done a brilliant job of formatting the book as well as putting promotional materials together.

I'd like to extend thanks to the beta readers and critique partners who have given me invaluable feedback at various stages of the process. Paul Mahlum, Gavin Jefferson, James Curcio, Andy Fletcher and Paul Loughman: you all had a hand in making this book the best it could be.

Thanks also to Natasha Snow for once again designing the perfect cover for the book, and to Dan Coxon of Momus Editorial for keeping the style and grammar tight. Both have been an absolute pleasure to work with.

Finally, I'd like to express my gratitude to everyone out there who has unknowingly provided the inspiration and encouragement to follow my vision.

ABOUT THE AUTHOR

C.R. Dudley is a visual artist, writer, and mind explorer. She is fascinated by the human condition, in particular the effect future technological developments might have on the psyche, and sees everything she creates as part of one continuous artwork.

She started blogging in 2014 as a way to express the ideas stemming from her studies in Jungian psychology, philosophy and various schools of mysticism. Her first few stories were distributed as hand-stitched art zines in aid of a mental health charity, and her style became known for its multi-layered narratives.

In 2017 she founded Orchid's Lantern, a small independent press focusing on the metaphysical and visionary genre. She is the author of short story collections *Fragments of Perception* and *Mind in the Gap*, as well as a forthcoming series of novels inspired by the unconscious mind.

C.R. Dudley lives in North Yorkshire and is a lover of forest walks, pizza, tequila and dark music.

Containing 36 mind-bending stories, *Fragments of Perception* will take you on a roller coaster ride through the depths of the psyche. In these imagined versions of our world, future technology meets metaphysics, quantum theory blurs with spirituality, and insanity becomes a friend.

Here you will see through the eyes of personified thoughtforms, people who worship black holes, and individuals exploring planes of shared consciousness. You will encounter guardian angels who feel misunderstood, meditating robots, and mythical species sending advice to humanity in unconventional ways.